THE BARKS & BEANS CAFE
MYSTERY SERIES

SHADE GROWN

THE BARKS & BEANS CAFE MYSTERY SERIES:
BOOK 8

HEATHER DAY GILBERT

FROM THE BACK COVER

Welcome to the Barks & Beans Cafe, a quaint place where folks pet shelter dogs while enjoying a cup of java...and where murder sometimes pays a visit.

During Lewisburg's popular summer home and garden tour, Macy and her brother Bo discover new aspects of their hometown's history. One of the last homes they visit features a lush commemorative shade garden marking where a Civil War soldier's bones were buried. As Macy pauses to admire a bed of blue hostas, she glimpses a shadowy shape lying beneath the dinner-plate leaves. It turns out to be the body of famed movie star Cody Franklin, who'd purchased the garden house as a quiet country retreat.

Back at the cafe, Macy speaks with Cody's distraught sister, who lets slip that she's afraid her brother's killer will target her next. Macy's heart goes out to the bereaved sibling, and she agrees to speak with Cody's local acquaintances in hopes she'll uncover some helpful backstory.

But someone powerful is lurking behind the scenes, and Macy has to zoom in on the killer before everything fades to black.

Join siblings Macy and Bo Hatfield as they sniff out crimes in their hometown...with plenty of dogs along for the ride! The Barks & Beans Cafe cozy mystery series features a small town, an amateur sleuth, and no swearing or graphic scenes. Find all the books at heatherdaygilbert.com!

The Barks & Beans Cafe series in order:
    Book 1: No Filter
    Book 2: Iced Over
    Book 3: Fair Trade
    Book 4: Spilled Milk
    Book 5: Trouble Brewing
    Book 6: Cold Drip
    Book 7: Roast Date
    Book 8: Shade Grown
    Book 9: Knight Brew
    Standalone Novella: House Blend

Dedicated to Susan Snodgrass, my loyal reader ever since my very first book, God's Daughter. At the time of her sudden passing this April, she had read every single one of my 23 books. She set a beautiful example of loving her husband and family, loving good books, and loving her Creator.

1

"Couldn't have asked for a better day for a home and garden tour." My brother Bo pushed his sunglasses up onto his red hair. He walked a couple of steps ahead of me on the buckling brick sidewalk.

I nodded, glancing at the sprawling brick house on our left. Bo was right—June was starting out well, with no humidity to speak of. Skies had been blue, and the sunlight hadn't yet gotten annoying with its intensity. With any luck, my three-story Colonial house wouldn't heat up until July, when Bo would have to haul my window-unit air conditioner out of my basement. Inevitably, my electric bills would get jacked up from that point.

We followed an older couple toward the next home on the tour—a well-kept gray Victorian with oversized planters of red begonias flanking both sides of the painted wooden porch.

As we stepped closer, I felt a familiar twinge of irritation to see Matilda Crump, the town busybody who, for reasons known only to her, maintained a fake British accent, even though she'd never resided in England. She sat behind a wrought-iron table near the front door, manning the garden club table that was piled with maps.

"Bo, Macy," she said crisply, her thick glasses shifting from my brother to me. "What a delight to see you here today." She gestured toward the front door. "There's nothing rubbish about this home, you'll find. Top-notch everything, renovated ten years ago. Be sure to note how the Greens have restored the original hardwood flooring throughout. Now, you will walk in and go directly to the right, then you'll make a circuit until you come round to the staircase."

"Are we able to go upstairs, too?" I asked. At the last place, the upper floor had been blocked off.

She fixed me with a patronizing smile. "And why wouldn't you go upstairs, pet?"

I didn't bother answering. The fact that she'd called me "pet" basically blew all my brain cells away.

As if sensing my vexation, Bo took my elbow and steered me forward a couple of steps. Shooting Matilda his most winsome smile, he said, "Thank you. It's been a lovely tour thus far."

A woman would have to be knocking at death's door to remain unaffected when my brother turned on the charm. He could be positively magnetic when he wanted to be. I often wished I would've inherited that ability. Instead, I'd received an extra helping of social awkwardness in my genetic code.

As a sudden gust of wind ruffled her frizzy salt-and-pepper hair, Matilda gave it a self-conscious pat and returned Bo's smile. "Excellent. And be sure to look in on the next tour home—the one with the memorial shade garden." She leaned in conspiratorially, clasping her wrinkled hands together as she lowered her voice. "You are aware that a Hollywood movie star—Cody something-or-other—lives in that house? You aren't allowed inside since it's under renovation. But the gardens out back are simply cracking."

Bo said, "We'd heard that. Thank you." He gave me another nudge, so I stepped into the cool darkness of the sitting room.

"I hadn't heard about the Cody something-or-other," I said, examining an antique grandfather clock.

"Didn't I tell you? City Council has been buzzing about it." He stepped toward the fireplace, where an old rifle had been framed in a glass box. "That's a Civil War Spencer rifle," he murmured, awe in his tone.

I walked over to him, glancing at the black baby grand piano parked in front of the bay window. "No, you haven't told me. Cody who?"

"Only Cody Franklin, one of the biggest stars today," he said, his gaze still riveted to the rifle.

"Cody Franklin? You're kidding me. Isn't he the one Summer's always talking about?"

At this, Bo whirled around. "She's talking about him?"

This past December, Summer and Bo got engaged. Summer runs the animal shelter, and she handpicks shelter dogs to bring to the "Barks" section of our Barks & Beans Cafe. Since Summer and I talk about everything, I'd just assumed she'd mentioned her crush on Cody Franklin to Bo by this point—after all, it was hard to find a blockbuster movie the guy *didn't* star in these days.

But now my brother was looking at me like I'd stabbed him in the heart. I rarely saw this jealous side of him, so I instantly repented of my faux pas, especially since his first fiancée had dumped him. I hadn't considered the fact that he might still be traumatized by Tara's ruthless—and completely ungrounded—rejection, but apparently he was.

"Oh, I just meant...maybe she told me she liked his movies," I said.

Bo turned wordlessly and walked into the next room. I hoped I hadn't sucked all his enjoyment out of the tour.

He remained silent as we toured the spacious second floor, then we trooped down to the kitchen that released onto a back patio. Stopping beside a fountain that gurgled peacefully in a landscaped flowerbed, Bo took a deep breath and turned his sky-blue eyes on me. They were framed in red lashes, just like mine, only my hair was a blonde-red shade that had been described as "marmalade."

"It's okay. I can handle a little Hollywood competition," Bo joked. "It's just...I don't know. I started thinking about Tara."

Blast that girl. Her memories always seemed to intrude into Bo's life, even though he hadn't seen her for a couple of years. As far as I knew, she still lived in California, though she no longer worked at Coffee Mass, the coffee bean importer where Bo had served for years as vice president.

I was nonetheless grateful that she'd broken things

off, because she'd sent Bo spiraling back toward our home state of West Virginia. He'd promptly started renovations on the front half of our great-aunt Athaleen's house. Aware that I was reeling from an unexpected divorce, he recalled my lifelong penchant for dogs and asked me to come in as partner to manage the doggie section of his cafe brainchild—a place where people could relax by petting shelter dogs. The Barks & Beans Cafe had the most amicable business partnership imaginable—Bo and I had been leaning on each other since we were small, when we'd lost our parents to a creek flood.

I placed a hand on his strong arm. "Tara's in the past. You have to stay focused on the *now*—on Summer, who loves you like crazy and is completely committed to you, just like you are to her. You and I are loyal people—we learned that from Auntie A—but Summer matches your loyalty, believe me. She's probably scouring the internet for bridesmaid dresses as we speak, since it seems to be her new favorite pastime." I grimaced, thinking of the fluffy coral monstrosity she'd sent me the link for yesterday. Thank goodness I was honestly able to tell her that coral was a no-go color for me. "No actor could ever usurp you," I added.

"I know you're right." He offered a hand so I could scramble over a worn-down dip in the sidewalk. "I just have to keep telling myself that."

2

We turned onto a tree-shaded pathway that led toward the back of Cody's house, which was clearly under renovation, given the loose boards piled on the front porch and the metal trash bin out front. But the front flowerbeds were lovely, filled with multi-colored phlox.

A woman with a cloud of fluffy white curls sat in a wheelchair behind a table. She greeted us with a friendly smile.

"What gorgeous flowers," I said, pointing to the bouquet of stunning burgundy daylilies and bright yellow irises that adorned the middle of the table.

"Aren't they, though?" she said. "Cody's manager brought those out this morning, along with the table. We haven't yet gotten the privilege of seeing the star himself, though." She smiled at Bo. "Am I right in thinking you're the new mayor? There aren't too many redheads around, you know."

He reached out to shake her extended hand. "You're right. I'm Bo Hatfield, and this is my sister, Macy."

"I'm Opal Tustin. I've heard of your cafe, but haven't been able to visit it yet. We're delighted that the two of you could come today." She angled her wheelchair and pointed. "You'll want to continue down this path, which will open onto the back garden area. The memorial shade garden has a plaque in front of it, so it's not hard to locate. I'm not sure how much you've heard of the history of this garden?"

"Not really anything," I said.

A woman in her sixties with unnaturally red hair walked up behind us and took the empty folding chair next to Opal. "Don't let me interrupt you," she said.

Opal continued. "Two years ago, a researcher was looking into Civil War-era burial sites in town. He'd come across a diary entry by someone who'd lived in this spot. The homeowner had described a soldier's burial and a large stone they'd placed atop the body, so the town gave the go-ahead to dig near that stone. They found the bones of a Confederate soldier who'd gotten shot in the Battle of Lewisburg in 1862. You see, after their victory, the Yankees started piling bodies of the dead Confederates at the church. People in town were upset by the careless treatment of the fallen soldiers, so they banded together after dusk, hoping to steal some of the bodies and give them proper funerals. This man here was one of the dead soldiers stolen away. The garden club designed the shade garden as a memorial for him."

Most everyone in Lewisburg knew of the battle and of the subsequent fallout when the victorious Union soldiers took over the town. Sometimes I walked into a wooded area behind the library, where there was a cross-shaped mass grave commemorating the ninety-five unknown Confederate soldiers who had died that day.

"What an honor for him. Did they figure out his name?" I asked.

The red-haired woman nodded her head, her eyes brimming with tears. "Thank goodness, they did—it's Matthew Brewer. He doesn't have to be an unknown, like all the others, bless them." She dabbed her eyes with a tissue. "Excuse me for getting emotional. I had a relative who died in the Confederate army, and it's still difficult to think about. I'm Abigail Belcher, by the way —I'm the president of the home and garden club. It's so lovely to have you with us today, Mayor Hatfield."

"Thank you." Bo threw a glance over his shoulder at the line that was rapidly forming. "We'll head on in to see it, but thank you for telling us how the shade garden came to be."

We walked under a wooden arbor covered in deep pink climbing roses just starting to bud. I sucked in a breath at the sheer expanse of emerald green lawn that stretched out to a copse of tall evergreens. Along the sides of the yard, handmade wooden borders lined raised flowerbeds, and lush green leaves and ferns spilled over the edging. Delicate flowering trees were centerpieces in some of the beds, while fountains trickled away in others. A circle of chairs sat off toward one side, inviting visitors to "sit and stay a spell," as Auntie A would've said.

A woman a little way ahead of us was carrying a

tiny dog in her arms, and it started barking furiously. While its grating yips were hardly terrifying, she shushed her pet, saying, "Quiet, Walter, you might scare people."

I had to grin. Her diminutive, fluffy canine could hardly compare to my hundred and sixty-five pound Great Dane, Coal, which was partly why I didn't bring him along on tours like this. I'd seen the fearful looks in people's eyes as I walked him along the streets, even with his soft muzzle on. For people with a dog phobia, nothing I said could convince them that a dog so big—and so tall, because his head nearly came up to my chest—was just a loveable, bumbling baby who wouldn't hurt anyone unless they tried to harm me.

Walter continued his restless barking, which seemed vaguely aimed at the ground beneath him. The woman finally gave up and set him down, commanding him to "go potty."

But instead of taking a bathroom break on the lawn (which would hardly be a delight to tour-goers), Walter darted toward the memorial bed that was chock-full of dinner-plate sized hosta leaves. Blue hostas, yellow-streaked hostas—you name the hosta, and that bed had it.

Walter placed his front paws against the wooden barrier and stretched upward, like he was limbering up to vault into the leafy bed. Since his owner had started a conversation with another woman, I hurried closer, placing myself between the dog and the hostas. Walter eyed me suspiciously, as if I were thwarting his noble aspirations.

Bo ambled my way, giving me a raised-eyebrow look as if to ask, "What's next, sis?"

I glanced behind me. Maybe the wooden border would hold my weight if I settled onto it, effectively blocking the dog's upward path. My gaze traveled from the border to the memorial plaque to the hostas spilling over it.

But directly behind the plaque, several of the hosta plants had been strangely mashed down. Visually following the path of their mangled leaves, I saw something brown protruding from under a sprawling blue hosta.

I leaned in for a closer look. Walter gave a sharp bark, then started sniffing at my leg. Hopefully, he wouldn't decide he'd found the perfect place to relieve himself.

It didn't take long for me to realize that the brown leather object I was staring at was the tip of a shoe—to be more specific, an expensive loafer with a thin white sole. In a shadow to the right of that shoe, I could just make out another one.

A sick feeling roiled through my stomach—a sinking certainty of what I was looking at. Before I could call Bo over, Walter jumped onto my extended shin, propelling himself toward the wooden border wall.

The dog's daredevil move brought my brother running. He managed to catch the wriggling Walter in both arms before he hit the shade bed. As the tiny dog growled, Bo ignored him and stalked over to his preoccupied owner. He deposited the pet next to her feet and said, "Ma'am, there is a leash law in Lewisburg. Dogs are required to be on a leash when they're not on their own property. I figure you brought one along with you on this tour?"

Bo was using his "resistance is futile" tone, which, combined with his powerful stare, could not be disobeyed. The woman reluctantly dug a leash from her quilted tote and clipped it onto Walter's collar. She shot me a glare, as if I were the instigator of all her dog's unhappiness, then turned back to her conversation.

My brother headed over to me, concern in his eyes. "You okay? Did he scratch your leg? His claws could definitely use a trim."

I shook my head. "I'm fine. But Bo, there's something here." I pointed a shaky finger toward the loafers, which were most assuredly attached to a body.

Bo stepped in, pushing a couple of hosta leaves aside to get a better view. His face hardened into disaster mode, and, although he'd retired early, he was still a well-trained DEA agent at heart.

He turned and made a sweeping gesture with his arm. "Everyone out!" he shouted.

People started scrambling toward the entry path, and the line by the table scattered. As Bo leaned in toward the body, my gaze swept the garden. It had been completely vacated, save for one petite, ice-blonde woman standing in the circle of evergreens.

The woman, who was dressed in a tailored-looking khaki and white outfit, seemed to be staring at Bo, but she hadn't budged in response to his evacuation command. I took a step toward her, in case she hadn't heard him, but the moment I moved, she dashed out of sight, toward the back fence line.

Torn between whether I should pursue the mystery woman or find out who was lying beneath the hostas, I glanced at Bo. He was busy placing a stone on the over-sized leaves so he could get a better look at the body. Abigail was hurrying our way and asking what was going on.

Knowing Bo would explain, I rushed toward the trees, just in case the blonde was somehow connected with the body in the hostas. Although it was possible the loafer-wearer wasn't dead—maybe just passed out or hungover—I had a feeling that wasn't the case.

Stepping into the wooded area that was carpeted with soft brown pine needles, I could see that the woman must've cleared out. I examined the tall, wooden fence line, but couldn't make out any exit. Bo called me back, and as I walked his way, I noticed a loose board. Giving it a push, I realized that a small person—like the blonde—could shimmy out that way.

But why had she felt the need to bolt for it?

A police siren wailed in the distance, so I jogged back to the memorial bed. Abigail looked horrified, and Bo shook his head.

"He's dead, I'm afraid," he said quietly. "Charlie's on his way."

Charlie Hatcher was the local police detective and a close friend. Thankfully, the station wasn't far away.

Abigail twisted her hands. "Oh, dear. Oh, my. This will look so bad for the garden club." She threw a wild glance over her shoulder. "I need to wheel Opal over here—she doesn't even know what's going on!" She hurried toward the entry table.

Bo took a step closer. "I haven't told Abigail, but she doesn't even know the half of how bad this is. He inclined his head toward the bed. "That's Cody Franklin lying there."

3

I gasped at the news. "No way. You're certain it's Cody?"

Bo nodded. "I do recognize *some* movie stars, sis." He glanced down. "And, to make things worse, he has a bloodstain on his shirt."

"Maybe he was killed." I grabbed Bo's arm. "Listen, there was a blonde woman hanging out by the fence, watching you. When I went to check on her, she'd taken off—I think through a board in the fence."

"You'll need to tell Charlie," he said.

Abigail was pushing Opal's wheelchair our way, so Bo hurried over to help. As he parked Opal by the memorial garden, Detective Hatcher stepped into view, with a couple of officers in tow.

He waved as he came closer. "Bo, Macy...ladies. What do we have here?"

With a side look at the garden club ladies, Bo explained that he believed the man in the hostas was movie star Cody Franklin and that, given the bloodstain on his shirt, he might've met with foul play.

Both women gasped, and Abigail leaned against Opal's chair. The detective stepped in to take a closer look at the body. After taking photos of Cody at various angles, he walked our way.

He introduced himself before asking the women, "Could I please have your names, ladies?"

Opal answered first. "I'm Opal Tustin." She cast another glance at Cody's body, placing a wrinkled hand to her chest. "Good heavens. I didn't even think he was home today."

The detective pulled out a notepad and pen. "Could you tell me why you believed Mr. Franklin wasn't home?"

Opal gave a slow nod. "I assumed he was gone, because his manager met us outside this morning to give us instructions about the house. The public were not allowed inside because of the home renovation, he said. He brought us out a table and gave us some flowers, and he seemed quite kind. But we never saw Cody Franklin."

"What was this manager's name?" the detective asked.

Opal gave a bewildered shrug, and Abigail piped up. "I believe his name was Tobias, but I don't know his last name. I can call the visitor's center and get his contact information."

"If you wouldn't mind," Detective Hatcher said. "And you are...?"

She shook his extended hand. "Abigail Belcher, president of the home and garden club. Opal and I were in charge of the memorial garden tour today. Hang on just a minute and I'll get that name for you."

She turned and headed toward the table, presumably to retrieve her phone. The detective asked Opal, "Did anything unusual happen here today? Anyone seem to be acting strangely on the tour?"

Opal thought for a moment. Even though she was sitting in a patch of sunlight, she drew her crocheted cardigan tighter across her shoulders. "Well, early in the tour, there was one fellow who seemed a bit...intoxicated," she said. "He smelled quite bad and his clothes were rumpled. We allowed him into the garden, but Abigail kept a sharp eye on him the entire time. He went into the evergreen woods at the end of the yard, and he stayed there so long we worried he might've passed out. But soon after, he walked out and left through the front gate, so we didn't give him another thought."

The detective nodded and looked up from his notebook. "How would you describe the man?"

Before Opal could answer, Abigail hurried toward us. "The manager's name is Tobias Blum," she said breathlessly. "I have his phone number here, detective."

She handed over a town map with a number written on it, which he tucked into his notebook. "Thank you, Miss Belcher."

"I'm a missus," she said rather sternly, as if the detective were hitting on her.

I had to hide my grin. Detective Charlie Hatcher was a handsome man who looked younger than his fifty-something years. His steely gray hair was the perfect complement to his inquisitive hazel eyes. On top of that, he had a very disarming dimple in his cheek that showed up every time he smiled. But he was happily married, and I was certain he had no intention of hitting on Mrs. Belcher.

Taking her insinuation in stride, he said, "I was just asking if you all could provide a description of the inebriated man who took the garden tour today?"

Abigail bobbed her head. "I actually took a photo of him, in case he caused any trouble." She clicked on her phone and pulled up a picture. After zooming in on it, she pointed to a bulky man with a bald head, standing near the edge of the lawn.

The detective gave a slow blink. "Right. That was a good idea to take a picture." He shot Bo a loaded look that I didn't understand. "I'd better return to the scene, but thank you for your time and information today, ladies. The tour is over for today, at least at this house. I'll get in touch with you again, if need be."

Opal picked up on his hint to clear out. "Thank you, detective. Abigail, would you mind wheeling me home?"

Bo offered to help, but Abigail said that Opal lived up a nearby side street less than ten minutes away. Once the ladies had moved out of earshot, the detective turned to Bo.

"Think it's him?" he asked.

"Could be—it's hard to tell from that blurry photo, and he was wearing a jacket, so I couldn't see if there was an anchor tattoo on his forearm. But I thought he skipped town last time he was caught dealing."

Of course my brother would be aware of any drug dealers in the area.

"I did, too. Haven't seen hide nor hair of him for years," the detective said.

Since I was clearly out of the loop as to who the man was, I placed my own cards on the table. "Charlie, I saw a woman standing by the fenceline when Bo told everyone to clear out. She was just lurking around, watching Bo. But before I could get to her, she high-tailed it away—I think she must've slipped behind a loose board." I pointed to the far left side of the fence. "It was over that way. She was short and thin with pale blonde hair, and she looked well put-together."

The detective wrote down what I'd shared. "Thanks, Macy. I'll have one of my officers check that board for prints." With that, he gave us a dismissive wave and headed over to join his men.

Bo heaved a sigh. "Well, this wasn't exactly the way I'd planned on wrapping up our home and garden tour. I could use some kind of pick-me-up—how about you? You want to go over to the General Lewis and get some of those free cookies and tea?"

"Even better, let's just order an early lunch there," I said. "I still remember those Norwegian-style eggs I had for brunch that one time."

"You're always a sucker for salmon," Bo said. "Sure, sis. Brunch it is."

As we walked to the General Lewis Inn, Bo elaborated on Cody's injuries, since I'd only gotten a look at the actor's expensive shoes.

"I've seen gunshot wounds before, and I feel certain

that's what Cody has, given the dark hole punched into his shirt pocket," Bo said. "But his bleeding pattern wasn't what I would've expected from a gunshot. There wasn't enough blood."

"I'm sure they'll figure it out in the autopsy," I said. "Hopefully, Charlie will keep you posted as to what they find."

"Without a doubt," he said. "And not just because I'm the mayor, although we'll probably have to find a way to spin this story so it doesn't reflect poorly on our town. That bald man in Mrs. Belcher's photo looked like a guy known as 'Boss Hogg' who used to sell drugs in our area. He hasn't been seen in a couple years, so I don't know why he'd return to a place where he'd get recognized, much less show up on a home and garden tour."

"Boss Hogg?" I asked. "As in, *The Dukes of Hazzard* Boss Hogg?"

Bo nodded. "That's the one. Might as well take his inspiration from a character who's crooked as a dog's hind leg, I suppose."

We arrived at the inn, stepping onto a boxwood-lined walkway as we made our way to the front door. The General Lewis was an impressive white building which had been built in the 1800s, although it had since been added onto. Under a flat, pillared roof, the inn's wide front porch was dotted with round tables, allowing restaurant visitors to dine outside.

Vibrant pink hydrangeas had been nestled into large pots atop the stairs, and the doorway was flanked by shaped evergreens in concrete planters. As we stepped into the shady coolness of the foyer, Bo suggested we eat outside, so we could keep an eye on what was going on in town.

The hostess led us to a corner table on the porch, where a bouquet of fresh wildflowers graced the crisp white tablecloth. We did have a good view of the main street, so I figured Bo would relax a little to know he wouldn't miss anything if were any further commotion. Although he hadn't actively sought his mayor position, once he'd gotten into it, he was one hundred percent committed.

As we sipped our coffee, I tried to take Bo's mind off the shocking death of a movie star on his hometown turf. "I can't believe I'm forty now," I said. "But somehow I do feel it."

He chuckled. "Get back to me when you catch up to my age. I'm nearly tipping into the next decade here at forty-four."

"Don't be so dramatic," I said. "You get better looking as you age. I don't think I'll be as lucky."

"I figure your boyfriend Titan would beg to differ," he said. "Anyway, we both got those Hatfield genes...whatever that means. I always figured they were tied to the red hair somehow."

"Maybe, but you know there are Hatfields with all hair colors. Remember that one Hatfield McCoy reunion festival we went to?" I laughed. "Next time, I should take Titan since he's one of those dread McCoys. We'll show everyone what this peace is all about."

Bo smiled, but he was still a little tight around the lips. I tried another tack. "Am I the only one who finds it ironic that you and Summer are getting married in October? I mean, her name is *Summer*, after all."

His gaze sharpened. "You aren't keen on an October wedding?"

I had to finish chewing before I answered, since I'd cut myself a precise bite of the hollandaise-covered poached egg, smoked salmon, and English muffin. "Of course I'm keen on it—I think it's perfect for you two. It's just a long stretch to wait, that's all."

He leaned back in his chair and took a sip of ice water. "The little church Summer wants to get married in doesn't have air conditioning, so we figured it'd be best to wait until fall. Things are less hectic then, anyway."

He shielded his eyes against the glare from the sun, watching the front walk. "Isn't that—"

"It's Charlie," I confirmed. I could see better from my side of the table.

We both fell silent until the detective caught sight of us. He headed straight toward our table. "Turns out, Cody's manager is staying here," he said. "I need to let him know what's happened."

Bo nodded, and Charlie headed into the foyer. Even though we'd both finished our food, we sat in apprehensive silence until the detective returned to the porch. This time, he was accompanied by a short man with curly black hair I had to assume was the manager, Tobias.

As Tobias walked down the steps, he pulled his phone out, and by the time he reached the boxwood-lined walkway, he was talking on it. His loud, agitated voice drifted our way.

"That's right. I hate to tell you. I can't believe it myself. I'm coming over to pick you up, then we'll go to the police station so they can fill us in."

As he strode out of view, Bo and I exchanged glances. "I wonder who he was talking to," I said. I absently flipped my phone over, then let out a low whistle. "It's nearly one. I need to get back and let Coal out before I head into the cafe for my afternoon shift."

"I forgot you were on duty today," he said. "You go on, and I'll get the bill."

"You always do. I work, too, bro."

"But I'm the one who retired early and is sitting on the 'money buckets,' as you call it. Let Daddy Warbucks pay this time."

I laughed. "You're hilarious, but you also have a point. Thanks—I'll see you tomorrow for church."

My brother picked me up every Sunday morning, rain or shine. He always arrived at least fifteen minutes early, even though our church was only five minutes away. He said it was a force of habit, since Auntie A had always taken us places early, but I knew it had more to do with him familiarizing himself with any given environment before anyone else did. I didn't know if it was a Marine technique or a DEA technique or just a Bo-keeping-the-upper-hand-in-all-situations   technique, but I tended to thwart his plans because I was rarely ready ahead of time. It was something I was working on, even though Bo seemed to be the only person affected by my dilly-dallying.

I hooked my purse over my shoulder and headed for home, relishing the fresh air. I glanced down the sidewalk leading to Cody Franklin's house, only to see that a couple of local news cars had already parked outside. The movie star's untimely death would soon bring in national media outlets, which would shake our small community.

Bo was right to be worried about how this would reflect on Lewisburg. A Hollywood star had moved here, probably hoping for a quieter life, and he'd wound up dying in his own back garden. Whether the person who'd killed him had been local or not, there was no way to spin the gruesome discovery of his body during the home and garden tour.

Mayor Boaz Hatfield would have his hands full in days to come.

4

I anticipated that Coal would be ready to race into the yard the moment I unlocked my back door, so I stepped aside when I opened it.

Sure enough, my black Dane gave me a passing sniff, then charged down the steps and onto the grass. He had business to do, and I was no part of it. I chuckled and headed inside, knowing he'd give a delicate scratch at the bottom of the screen door when he wanted back in.

My phone rang just as I was pulling a more comfortable shirt over my head. Bristol, the young woman who shared duties in the Barks section, was on the other end.

"Summer wanted me to ask if you'd mind bringing Coal in today. The shelter dogs—puppies, actually—are bored and whiny. She said Coal is good with the small ones."

Coal was good with tiny pets of any variety, since my brother's cat Stormy had trained him into submission. With bigger dogs, like my neighbor's dog Waffles, he tended to get more territorial.

"Of course. I'll bring him when I come over, in about fifteen minutes. What's the story with the puppies?"

"Summer said their mother was hit by a car, so they were left homeless in the grocery store parking lot." She paused as one of the puppies gave a loud whine. "They're some kind of Chihuahua mix, so they're miniscule. I have to watch to make sure they don't dart under my feet. They're called 'Pip' and 'Squeak' for the time being."

"Sounds like the perfect names." I put in gold hoop earrings. "How's your packing going for college?"

Bristol was heading to Maryland at the end of August, since she'd gotten into a competitive Graphic Design program and had finally saved up enough to go. Bo and I had sent a large anonymous donation to help her out, but we didn't look forward to replacing her in the cafe. Our barista Milo was going to miss her, too, since they'd been dating on and off for months. Hopefully, they would stay in touch with each other.

"It's going all right. I'm not actually sure how much I'll need to take, though, since I'll have a roommate. Hopefully she'll get back to me as to whether she has a mini fridge, coffeemaker, or bigger items like that."

"I'm sure she will." I swiped mascara over my lashes. "Okay, I'll be over in a few."

I hastily ran a comb through my thick waves, hoping to tamp them into some kind of recognizable style. After putting on a coat of nude lipstick, I headed downstairs, slipped on Coal's muzzle and leash, and walked him through the connecting door into the cafe. Living so close to work—which was in the front section of the house I occupied—was handy, but for privacy's sake, I rarely used the connecting door.

As usual, I heard low-voiced exclamations the moment Coal stepped into the cafe. He was impossible to miss in all his sleek black glory, and I knew he looked like a giant next to me, since I only stood five foot three. He walked in a straight line toward the Barks section, like he was aware of his duty and he planned to perform it to the best of his ability.

We stepped into the doggie gate, which was attached to a low brick divider wall, and Bristol hurried our way. She was looking fresh as a daisy with her smooth skin, glossy dark hair, and cherry-red sweater perfectly fitted to her full-figured frame.

Two itty-bitty pups slowly trailed along behind her, whining as they went. She gave a little clap of her hands to hurry them over, but they hesitated when they saw Coal. Ever the genteel Dane, he obligingly lowered his front and back feet onto the floor and sat, waiting for them to approach him.

Bristol pointed to the closer one and said, "Pip's the mostly black one, and Squeak is more tan. Pip is a boy and Squeak is a girl, Summer said."

I smiled. "Hopefully they won't get stuck with those names." As they sniffed their way closer to Coal, Bristol asked, "Did you hear on the news that Cody Franklin was found dead in our town—you know, the movie star? I can hardly believe it. What was he doing here?"

I didn't know how much I should fill Bristol in, so I just nodded. "It's terrible."

"They're not saying how he died yet. I'm wondering if it wasn't an overdose or something—it seems like so many movie stars are dying that way nowadays."

I didn't want to launch into such a grim topic in front of our cafe guests, who were shifting in their seats to watch Coal as he interacted with the puppies. "I'm sure they'll release more details soon," I said.

Bending down, I gave Squeak a pet, since she'd sidled up to my leg. Meanwhile, Pip had settled in comfortably between Coal's giant front paws and was licking at his nose. A couple of people moved into the Barks section, since they'd realized Coal was every bit as gentle as he was huge.

Kylie walked over to join us. "We're having a lull over at the cafe," she said. "You heading home soon, Bristol?"

Bristol gathered up her jacket and bag. "I am. Mom's sitting with a hospice patient and Farrell's teaching a night class, so I'm on supper duty. Any ideas?"

"Maybe spaghetti?" Kylie suggested. "It always works in a pinch."

"Good idea. I have some garlic bread in the freezer, too. Have a good night, ladies." Bristol walked out, her blingy sandals flipping as she went.

Kylie glanced at Coal, who was now lying on the floor with Pip and Squeak crawling all over him. "What a dog," she sighed. "If only our tiny house had room for one. I'd get a German Shepherd."

I nodded. If I could match Kylie with a dog, it would definitely be something striking and intimidating, like a Shepherd.

"How's your sister?" I asked. I liked to keep tabs on her younger sister, Chelsea, who'd gotten into such a risky situation last year that we'd had to work together to extricate her from it.

"She's still working at the cell phone company. It turns out, she's quite the convincing salesperson—it's not hard for her to manipulate people." She laughed. "And don't I know it. She's still living with me."

That was the best place for her, in my opinion, given her rather flaky parents. "Good," I said.

Kylie ran a hand through her short, dark bob. She must've recently gotten a trim, because the dragon tattoo that ran up her neck was very visible. She'd probably be labeled Emo these days—if Emo was still a thing. Yet I knew that under all her edgy black clothing and lug-sole boots, she had a shining heart of gold, no matter how hard she tried to hide it. She was a protector like Bo, even though she tended to blur the lines and go more vigilante than he did.

She was the kind of person I'd want by my side in a pinch. I always felt safer having Kylie or Bo in the cafe.

She crouched down to pet Pip, who'd tumbled her way. "I'm ordering some really unique knives for the fall flea market this year. You should drop by and pick up something for Bo. When is his birthday again?"

"It's not till January. I could get him something for Christmas, though. Just do me a favor and don't sell a sword to anyone who plans to kill someone with it." I still had vivid memories of how one of Kylie's swords had been used to murder a man at last year's flea market.

She cringed. "You *would* have to bring that up,

wouldn't you?" Pulling up the leg of her black jeans, she pointed to a sword tattoo running up the side of her shin. "Have I showed you this new one? It's a memento that I survived a run-in with a murderer. You should get one, too."

If I got a tattoo for every murderer I'd met, my body would get covered fast. Besides, I hated needles almost as much as I hated the sight of blood. "No, thank you. But it looks great on you."

Shrugging, she gave Pip a final pat. The bell on the door jingled and two customers walked in—and one of them was Tobias, Cody's manager.

Kylie strode back to the coffee bar. I found myself hoping that Tobias would order one of Kylie's famed lattes, since I was positive her foam art surpassed anything he'd find at a Hollywood cafe. As Pip and Squeak took turns trying to "pin" Coal to the ground, I observed the woman who'd entered with Tobias.

She looked like a movie star herself, with long, thick hair a convincing shade of natural blonde, tan skin with a healthy glow, and jeans and a sweater that fit her perfectly. She had that kind of effortless chic that some women have, as if their stylish clothing and accessories materialized out of thin air when they rolled out of bed in the morning. Given how she towered over Tobias, I was guessing she was nearly six feet tall.

She turned to look at the dog section, and even her face was striking, with features that had the glamour of an old-school movie star. But her amused smile hinted that she was someone approachable, which would be a nice twist on your stereotypical Hollywood type.

Maybe an actress had accompanied Tobias for his stay at the inn?

As they picked up their orders, I was further heartened to see that the glam woman had chosen Charity's pork barbeque sliders with honey lime coleslaw. Tobias was toting a wide latte mug, so he had probably gotten a foam art drink. They'd be trying out the best we had to offer.

The woman led them toward a more private booth near the low divider wall. Tobias briefly placed his hand on the small of her back, but she sped up, effectively forcing him to drop it.

As they settled into opposite sides of the booth, Tobias seemed irritated, maybe because his advances had been rebuffed. But after taking a long sip of coffee, he launched into conversation.

"We'll have to finish renovations on his house first." He frowned. "Aspen, you and I both know he's invested way too much in that money pit. I almost stepped through a rotten floorboard on the stairs when I saw him last night."

Aspen swallowed a bite of sandwich. Her intelligent blue eyes widened. "You saw him last night? How late? I didn't hear you mention that to the police."

They must be discussing Cody Franklin. As I leaned in a bit closer, Coal shifted at my feet, then heaved himself into a standing position. He began to round the pups toward the play area, probably hoping they'd discover some toys and leave him alone.

"They didn't ask," Tobias said. "Anyway, it's not like I'm hiding anything."

Unobtrusively, I sat down in a round corner booth,

thus enabling myself to hear the nearby conversation, even though I couldn't see them talking.

Aspen didn't give him a quick response, so I guessed she was eating again. Then she said, "They told me he must've died early this morning, given his body temperature."

"I guess so, but I don't know why on earth he headed into that garden. Last night, I told him that everything was under control with the garden club. I explained that he'd need to leave the house by nine, so he could stay away from prying eyes. We were going to meet up at the French restaurant tonight...and you were supposed to meet us there, right?" He gave an exasperated huff. "Anyway, *you* were the one staying in the house with him. You would've known more about when he was coming and going than I did."

Hostility filled her tone. "I'm not my brother's keeper. He'd bought me a morning spa package at the Greenbrier, so that's where I was—getting a detox body wrap."

Cody must have been Aspen's brother. I was beginning to get a clearer picture of the relationship between these two.

And he must have been a generous brother, because The Greenbrier Resort's spa would be pricey. I was sure I wouldn't be able to afford a treatment there. Maybe that explained why Aspen's skin looked so dewy.

Coal gave a brief growl. I jumped to my feet, certain everyone would be looking to see if something was wrong.

But Coal was simply nudging Pip away from a

relentless attack on Squeak's tiny tail. What a peace-maker my Dane was.

A customer who'd been lingering by the dog gate smiled and walked in, so we talked a little before she headed over to pet the puppies. Maybe she'd find their frolicking antics endearing, or even consider taking one or both of them home.

Tuning back into the conversation behind me, I heard Tobias say, "He certainly had no problem throwing money around. I know your private flight from Nashville couldn't have been cheap."

Her voice lowered. "You're just jealous he didn't ask you to stay at the house with him, but you would've hated it, and he knew it. The rotting steps weren't the only danger zone, believe me. I'm betting you never even tried the upstairs toilet." She paused a moment. "Have you told Lizzie yet?"

I realized she must be referring to Lizzie Morris, Cody's ex-wife. She was an actress who was even more well-known than Cody was, if that were even possible.

Tobias snorted. "Are you kidding me? She'd be thrilled to know he's dead. They ended on bad terms—the kind of terms that make me sick. If I hadn't found a real shark of a lawyer, she would've taken him for all he was worth. And you know that's a substantial amount."

"Good thing you were protecting my brother's best interests." Aspen's dry tone belied her words. She stood and stretched, throwing a glance toward Coal. "What a gorgeous dog! I'm heading in there. Keep me posted."

"More like you keep *me* posted." Tobias dusted invis-ible crumbs from his dark pants. "I'm sure the police

will update you before they do me. I'm not even sure
how long I need to stick around."

"That detective said don't go anywhere until they
hear back on the autopsy, and he said those are backed
up in this state." She ran a hand through her bangs.
"That means I'll have to find another place to stay, since
the police are going over the house. How's your inn?"

"It's lovely, but at breakfast they told me it's booked
solid," he said.

Unable to remain quiet when I had the opportunity
to help a cafe guest, I stood from my seat. "I'm sorry, but
I couldn't help overhearing you're looking for a place to
stay. There's a great inn a little ways out of town. It used
to be called Baxter Manor, but it was taken over by new
management this February, and now it's called
Donovan Place. It has gorgeous landscaping, and
there's a chef onsite." I smiled at both of them. "I'm
Macy Hatfield, by the way. My brother and I own this
cafe. Anyway, my barista Milo's parents bought the inn,
and they've added some new amenities, like a sauna
and hot tub. From what I hear, they've only just started
advertising widely, so you'd probably be able to find a
room."

Tobias studied me, as if I were a rare curiosity in a
shop. I was probably over-explaining, as I tended to do
when I got nervous. But Aspen returned my smile and
stepped into the Barks section. "Sounds perfect. I'll look
it up."

Tobias shrugged at me, then offered a halfhearted
wave to Aspen. "Thanks for meeting up."

Coal lumbered toward Aspen, his tail wagging. He

stopped short in front of her, as if unsure if she'd want to pet him.

"That one's mine," I said. "He likes you."

She gave him a pat on the head, then rubbed behind one of his permanently pricked ears. They'd been cropped when he was a puppy, before I'd adopted him from the shelter. I'd actually had people lecture me on the dangers of ear cropping, as if it had ruined him for life. Each time, I would politely explain that I'd had nothing to do with the decision, all the while thinking they needed to find something better to do with their time than to criticize something that could never be undone anyway.

Sometimes I wished I were more like Bo, who would've told them in no uncertain terms to mind their own business. But random strangers seemed to feel compelled to talk to me. Apparently, I didn't radiate the same "keep your distance" vibes my brother did.

Case in point: Aspen was currently grumbling about how uptight Tobias was. "He's a good manager, though," she added, almost to herself. Coal sat down and thumped his tail as if in agreement, and she gave him another pat.

It seemed as good a time as any to share that I knew who she was. "I gathered that you're Cody Franklin's sister, and that Tobias is—I mean, was—his manager," I said. "I just want to say I'm so sorry about what happened. I was actually the one who found him on that garden tour. Please let me know if there's any way we can make your stay easier while you're in town. You can call the cafe anytime and ask for Macy."

She eased into a nearby chair, likely exhausted from

the shock of this morning. "You're so kind—thank you."
She looked absently out the large windows lining the
exterior wall. "I was afraid Cody was running with a fast
crowd, but I thought he'd grow out of it. Granted, he
was twenty-eight and I'm only twenty-three, but I've
always felt like our roles were somehow reversed. I was
the old soul who didn't break any rules, and he was the
rebel who was determined to live life to the fullest."

As I sat down next to her, Squeak came running
over and sniffed at my ankle. I ran a hand over her
tawny fur and asked, "What do you mean by a 'fast
crowd?'"

"Drugs," she said simply. "I thought by coming here,
he'd get away from that life and kick his addictions for
good. He told me he'd cleaned up his act." Her flashing
eyes met mine. "But now I find myself wondering if his
entire house renovation was some kind of cover to meet
with an east coast dealer." She sighed. "So much for the
idyllic small-town mountain life."

5

Much as I wished I could alleviate Aspen's cynicism about the small-town drug trade, I really couldn't. Since we knew Boss Hogg might've been on the garden tour—in Cody's back yard, no less —there could have been a drug connection in her brother's death.

"I'm sorry," I said.

She nodded, but seemed lost in thought, so I fell silent.

Coal stood and nudged Squeak away from my ankles. He plopped down in front of me, as if claiming his own territory. Effectively shunned by her big mentor, Squeak ran directly toward Pip and attempted to steal a ball from his mouth.

"Now look what you did," I whispered to Coal.

Aspen glanced at her phone. "I'd better make a reservation at that Donovan Place. I'm not sure how long I'll have to stay there, but I don't feel like Cody's house would be safe. What if the person who...well, what if they came after me?"

I scrambled to reassure her. "I can't see why anyone would target you, especially if your brother's death was drug-related."

"I know, but I can't even be sure of that." She looked thoughtful. "He didn't act like he was using, although I know it can sometimes be hard to spot. He did seem kind of reclusive living here, but I just figured he didn't want to be accosted by fans in town." She shivered and rubbed her arms, even though the cafe temperature was comfortable. "What if there's someone he didn't want to run into? And what if that person finds me? I don't even know who to watch out for."

She seemed to be getting a little paranoid about her brother's death, but I couldn't blame her. If someone had shot Bo (God forbid!), I would move heaven and earth to find out who did it.

"I'll tell you what," I said. "I grew up here, so I have a lot of connections in town. I can look into things, maybe see if Cody was talking to someone in particular before he died." I sat up straighter, and Coal responded with a whine, as if he were ready to get back to his comfy pillow at home. Rubbing his head, I mused, "I wonder if Cody's contractor would've noticed him meeting with anyone."

Aspen snapped her fingers. "His contractor is this guy with some pretentious name, like 'Governor' or something."

I rolled my eyes. "Chancellor. It has to be Chancellor Huddnall."

"That's the one!" she said eagerly. "Do you know him?"

"Handsome and cocky?" I asked. "I think everyone knows Chancellor."

She nodded. "When I first got to town, he hit on me about as tactfully as a runaway train barreling down the tracks."

"He's pretty predictable that way," I said. "But I can handle him. Do you think he'll keep up the construction work when the police give the all-clear?"

"He's planning to. He called to ask me if he'd still get paid for the job, so I told him to keep going with it. It makes sense to finish the house, even though I'll probably sell it, since I have no plans to live in West Virginia." She held up a palm. "No offense, of course. It's a beautiful place, but I'm more of a city girl."

"I understand. It's not for everyone." I thought of Tara, who never would've fit in here. The mountains were a comfort to those who belonged here and a curse to those who didn't.

Aspen stood. "You've really gone above and beyond to help me, Macy. I can't thank you enough." She pulled out her phone, touched the screen a couple of times, then handed it over to me. "You want to plug your cell number in for me? And I'll share mine."

"Sure." I opened my contact list, then passed my phone to her. "And I'm serious when I say to call me if you need anything. My brother's a great cook, and he always has leftovers."

She grinned. "Thank you." As Pip and Squeak raced toward us, she said, "I wish I could take one of these cuties with me, but my apartment only allows cats. I guess they've had problems with dogs in the past." She walked out the dog gate and gave me a parting smile. "We'll talk soon."

Hopefully, the next time we talked, I would've gleaned some information that could put her restless mind at ease.

SUNDAY MORNING ROLLED IN GENTLY, with the steady hum of rain on my windows. I took it easy in my PJs, relaxing with a cup of our Costa Rican house blend on my couch. As if sensing the slower pace, Coal climbed up to sit next to me, resting his face on the side of my leg. Occasionally, he threw shamelessly adoring glances at me, making me feel like I was the only one on earth he truly loved.

Sometimes I wondered if any man could ever be as unceasingly loyal and sacrificial as a dog. Of course, I was jaded after my divorce from Jake (the Snake). I wanted to believe that Titan would never let me down like Jake had; that he would continue to look at me like I hung the moon. It seemed likely that he would.

But, as I'd told him again recently, I wasn't ready to remarry yet. No matter how loving and healthy our relationship was, a sliver of doubt always stabbed at my thoughts of marrying again. I wasn't sure when or how I would eliminate that sliver, but until then, I couldn't say yes to a lifelong commitment.

Titan was also a divorcee, but he wasn't hesitant to take the next step. His family supported our relationship—even encouraged it. His two older sisters had taken a liking to me based on my description alone, conveniently ignoring my Hatfield last name. They'd invited me to several family events, but I'd wriggled out of each one since I knew what would happen if I went.

I'd fall for Titan's family like I'd fallen for him, that's what.

THE RAIN STOPPED AFTER CHURCH, so I walked Coal over to Bo's. He lived just a couple houses up from mine in a beachy, bungalow-style home. I opened his ocean-blue front door and walked in, since he always left it unlocked when I was coming over.

I inhaled the welcoming scents of beef roast and fresh bread as Bo turned from his kitchen counter. He hadn't changed out of his plaid button-up and chinos, and he'd tied on the cutesy, heart-covered apron Summer had given him for his birthday that said "Kitty Daddy." The outlandishness of such an item on my tough brother never failed to bring a grin to my face.

"Hey, sis, you can just relax on the couch," he said. "I only have to cut the roast and grab the rolls. Summer should get here soon."

I nodded, throwing a look at his calico Stormy. She was sitting atop her cat tower, giving Coal a narrow-eyed stare. Flipping her fluffy, multicolored tail in our direction, she casually raised her front paw and began licking it to clean her head.

As if he knew the routine, Coal padded into the living room and sat down, pretending not to notice

Stormy. I sank onto the couch behind him and gave his head a pat. "You're a good boy," I whispered.

A light knock sounded on the door, and Summer came in, looking like some kind of water sprite. She wore a blue-and-green swirled skirt and dangling earrings to match. Her honey-colored hair looked windswept, and she had bracelets stacked up both fore-arms. The only things that hinted she'd come out of a Mennonite background (which she refused to talk about) were her long hair and lack of makeup.

After kicking off her gold sandals, she headed straight for Bo, wrapped her arms around him, and gave him a kiss on the cheek.

He colored a bit under his freckles, but joked, "Hey, I'm trying to get some work done here."

She gave him a haughty pat on the shoulder. "I'll leave the chef alone, then. For now." She headed over to greet me. There was something comforting about her dark brown eyes, which always seemed to see into my deeper motivations without judging me.

She glanced at Stormy, who had grabbed a tiny stuffed mouse and was now silently inching her way toward Coal. Jabbing her thumb toward the calico, Summer said, "That cat has so much attitude. The other day, she literally meowed and meowed for me to pet her, then when I reached down, she swatted my hand and stalked away."

I gave a snort. "She's just jealous. She wants to be the only girl in Bo's life."

"Don't we all," Summer joked. She sat down in a chair across from me.

"What happened to Pip and Squeak?" I asked. "They were so adorable."

"I know. But they didn't get adopted. I dropped them off at the cafe before I came here, hoping someone might notice them today, even though the Sunday hours are limited. If there's no interest, I'll probably bring them in tomorrow, too, since we're actually low on dogs right now—can you imagine? But we've had an explosion of cats. I don't suppose you—"

"No cats for me," I said. "I prefer to watch Stormy from afar. Every time I pet-sit her in my house, disasters occur."

"Oh, yeah—the flooded laundry room incident," Summer said ruefully. "Well, Stormy was a bit wild, even as a kitten." She leaned closer. "Bo told me you all were at Cody Franklin's place when you found him lying there. Did you see his sister? I heard she's been spotted in town."

"You really do keep up on your Cody trivia, don't you?" I winked. "Actually, she visited the cafe yesterday, and we talked some. She's quite nice. I couldn't say the same about her brother's manager Tobias. He seemed more big-city prickly."

Summer's eyes widened. "I can't believe you met Aspen. Rumor has it she just got cast in a big-budget movie as the lead actress. It'll be her first time acting, but they say she's a natural."

This surprised me, because Aspen hadn't hinted that she was leaving Nashville anytime soon. "Interesting," I said.

Summer's eyes seemed to drill into mine. "Hang on.

You know something more about Aspen, don't you? Something you're not telling me."

I glanced over at my brother, who was arranging a salad on the table. Lowering my voice to a whisper, I said, "She was worried about what happened to Cody. I told her I'd look into people in town for her." I angled my head at Bo. "But he doesn't need to know."

Summer's lips twisted. "I don't think—"

"Time to eat," Bo announced, a wide smile on his face. "Get it while it's hot!"

Stormy stopped short at the sound of Bo's voice, as if she'd been caught red-handed. She hurriedly sidled up to Coal and dropped her mouse between his paws. He stared at it as if it were a hot potato he had no intention of touching.

"Coming!" I shouted back, leveling a stare at Summer that said, "Do not tell my big brother about my undercover operations."

She heaved a sigh, but gave me a quick nod before standing. "I can't wait to taste those homemade rolls," she said cheerfully, walking over and giving Bo another hug.

spen texted Monday morning to let me know she was enjoying her stay at Donovan Place. "They literally had ten things to choose from for the breakfast buffet. I stuffed myself on Belgian waffles. Also, the police opened Cody's house, so Chancellor's back at work today, in case you wanted to talk with him."

I didn't really *want* to talk with the Don Juan of contractors, but I figured he'd be more open with me than with the distractingly beautiful Aspen—who'd now become his boss by default.

On my lunch break, I headed home, knowing Coal would enjoy a walk through town. Once I'd put on his soft muzzle and leash, I led him toward Cody's street, enjoying the sunshine and the smell of fresh-cut summer grass.

A giant blue dual-wheeled truck was parked directly in front of the house. The pieces of wood in the truck bed told me it probably belonged to Chancellor, as did the sounds of drilling and hammering escaping the windows.

I made a clicking sound, so Coal would return to my side before we stepped onto the front porch. I pressed the doorbell button, but when nothing happened, I gave it a good rap. I wasn't sure if anyone could possibly hear me given the levels of noise inside, but a couple of minutes later, I heard boots thudding my way.

Chancellor opened the door, taking a long moment to look me up and down. "Why, if it isn't Macy Hatfield. You can come on in." He looked at Coal. "Not your dog, though."

"I'd rather talk out here." I felt less of an exhibit with my big Dane at my side, and things were quieter on the porch, anyway.

"Sure. What can I do ya for?" He stepped out, blowing at a strand of long, glossy black hair that had escaped the braid running down his back. His lips turned up in their perpetual smirk.

It was impossible for Chancellor Huddnall to go unnoticed. Thanks to his direct Cherokee ancestry, he had striking black eyebrows and a smoldering dark gaze. He was in his mid-thirties, but could pass for someone in his twenties, and he knew it. Women seemed to fall like dominos around him.

But not this woman, and I needed to make sure he knew it. Though he was acting suave, his gaze had darted toward Coal one time too many. He was scared of my dog, and I didn't mind capitalizing on that fact. I took a step back, so Coal wound up standing closer to him than I did.

"How are things coming along with this place?" I asked.

He shrugged. "Fair to middlin', as they say. At least there aren't foundation problems, but Mr. Franklin wanted to salvage the original wood floors, so that's a tedious process." He rested a hand on the doorframe, striking a casual pose. "He also wanted to keep the plaster walls, but I told him those are a nightmare. There aren't many good plasterers these days. I'm hoping to talk her—his sister, I mean—into drywall." He gave me a too-friendly smile. "She's an actress, you know. But not as pretty as you are by a long mile."

I pulled out my other secret weapon to defuse his interest. "You know, Bo and I found Cody in that back garden. It was horrible."

Chancellor's eyes widened on mention of Bo's name. As I'd suspected, he'd forgotten who my brother was. It was only right to give him a little reminder.

He stood straighter. "Oh, yeah. Terrible stuff. They're saying he got shot."

"They haven't released many details yet. Were you working that day? I didn't notice you around."

"Nah, those old ladies didn't want us making any racket—disturbing the garden vibes, you know? My crew and I were off." He made eye contact with Coal, who'd been watching him like a hawk, and gave him a strained smile.

"Makes sense." I needed to put him more at ease, so I tugged on Coal's leash. His amber eyes met mine, as if asking if I really wanted this, and I tugged again. He backed up and sat down. "What did you think of Cody —I mean, Mr. Franklin?" I asked. "Was he the friendly type, or more of a loner? I didn't see him in town much. I don't think he ever visited the cafe."

Chancellor considered my question. "He didn't have many friends, I'd say. He stuck around here Friday nights, when most single guys would go out. Maybe he didn't want to get recognized." He frowned. "There was this one guy who came here my third day on the job, though. Some big bald dude, pushing his way into the house, threatening Mr. Franklin that he'd better pay up. It got me worried. If he wasn't paying people, maybe he wouldn't pay me, you know? But I asked him about it, and he said if I checked my account, I'd see he'd already paid me for the previous days' work. I did, and sure enough, the money was there. He must've paid me that morning."

"Did you ever see that bald guy again?" I asked.

"No." As one of his men yelled from upstairs, he gave me an apologetic look. "I'd better get back to business. It was nice talking, though. If I think of anything else, I'll call you. What's your number?"

It was sneaky how he slipped that in, but there was no way I was giving him my personal cell. "You can reach me at the cafe—just leave a message if I'm not there."

He gave me a disappointed nod. "Will do."

As he turned to go, I recalled Bo's description of the drug dealer. Taking a wild stab in the dark, I asked, "Did you happen to notice if the bald guy had any tattoos?"

Chancellor whirled around, another hair escaping his shiny braid. "Funny you should ask. He had a tattoo on his arm—not a quality tat, either. Kinda faded. It was an anchor." He gave me a suggestive smile. "If you're into tattoos, I have some good ones. Play your cards right, and I can show you someday."

I gave a short cough, attempting to cover the scornful laugh bubbling up inside me. Pulling Coal up closer, I leveled my gaze at the bold lothario. "I don't think so."

With a halfhearted wave, Chancellor skulked off into the house.

Coal tugged on his leash. I followed him down the sidewalk, only too happy to put as much distance between me and the irritating contractor as possible.

BY THE TIME we got to the cafe, I was able to chuckle about my encounter with Chancellor. It helped to picture him having a run-in with Titan, my six-foot-five, FBI agent boyfriend. I knew exactly how that would go.

Throw my brother into the mix, and you could charge money for the show.

After letting Coal take a bathroom break, I decided to bring him into the cafe again. Pip and Squeak were once again in the Barks section, along with an older dog, Ralph, who kept pretty much to himself. I figured Coal would enjoy the interaction and Ralph would enjoy the break from the tumbling pups.

My barista Jimmy greeted me as I walked in, calling me over to hand me one of the new dog treats our baker Charity had cooked up. "Try this on for size, big boy," he said to Coal, giving him an affectionate head pat.

I took Coal's soft muzzle off, then handed him the coffee-cup shaped treat. He took it delicately between his huge teeth, then sat down to munch on it.

Since there were no customers in line, I decided to bring up Boss Hogg. Jimmy used to be a high school bus driver, so he knew many of the people in town.

"Did you ever hear of a bald guy with an anchor tattoo?" I asked him.

Jimmy creased his wide brow. "Can't say that I have. I could ask Jenny for you."

Jenny was Jimmy's wife, and together, they made a complete unit. I couldn't imagine one without the other.

Before I could answer, Charity stepped out of the back room, a wet dishtowel in her hands. Her rosy cheeks were more flushed than usual, contrasting with her thick crown of white curls. Her cherubic face made her resemble Mrs. Claus, and she cared for children every bit as much. She'd adopted her grandson Roman just last year, and he was thriving under her watchful care. She'd worked hard with him so he could enter kindergarten this fall, even though his developmental delays had already put him a year behind everyone else.

"I heard you asking about that tattooed man," she said. "Now, Macy, you don't want to go there." A concerned edge crept into her soft blue eyes.

Coal licked his lips, and I leaned in closer. "Charity, what do you know about him?"

She gave a sigh. "Come here." She waved me into the back room, so I slipped Coal's muzzle on and followed her in.

She turned away from me, arranging her towel over the metal bar on the sink. "A bald man with an anchor tattoo came to our home years ago. He was looking for my son, Brian." She faced me again, tears welling in her eyes. "He said he was a friend of Brian's, but I knew that wasn't true. He was looking for payment for drugs, which Brian had gotten into. I grabbed the baseball bat we kept behind the door and told him to leave and never come back."

I couldn't imagine the peaceable Charity doing such a lionhearted thing, but then again, Boss Hogg should've known not to mess with a mom.

She frowned. "He dug in, refusing to leave until he got his money. Thankfully, my Milt was around then, and he came up behind me." I'd already gathered that Charity's deceased husband had loved and supported her. "He told that son of a biscuit-eater that if he ever showed up again, he would make sure he didn't even get a chance to ring the doorbell."

I tried not to smile at Charity's "biscuit-eater" term, which I was sure I'd heard Auntie Athaleen use at some point. "So that was how many years ago—do you remember?"

She scrunched up her eyes and tapped a finger to her lip. "Let me see...it must've been nigh on twelve years or more. I haven't seen that baldie in these parts since, but I always carry a knife on me, just in case." She patted her pants pocket.

I was seeing an entirely new side of our gentle baker. Even though she didn't look dangerous, like Kylie, she certainly wasn't a woman to be trifled with.

Coal gave a subtle sniff, probably ready to head over

to the puppies. I rubbed behind his ear. "Thanks for telling me that, Charity. I appreciate it."

She grabbed my arm. "Macy Jane Hatfield, you'd better promise me you won't go looking for trouble with that man."

I had no idea she knew my middle name. We'd asked our employees to call us "Miss Hatfield" and "Mr. Hatfield," and up until now, Charity had done so. This was definitely personal to her.

"I'm not looking for trouble, I promise." I glanced at the clock on the wall, noting we'd gone five minutes past my lunch break. "I'd better get back to the dogs."

She relaxed her fearsome grip on my arm. After working up a convincingly cheerful smile, she said, "Take care of yourself."

She clearly meant it as a command, so I gave her hand a squeeze. "I will."

Her blue gaze sharpened. "Oh yes, indeedy, you surely will."

7

C oal rolled onto his back on the doggie mat, tongue lolling out as if he were utterly relaxed. Yet the gaze he turned on Pip and Squeak was intense. He wanted to play, and he was hoping they'd catch on.

Sure enough, Pip strutted over first, his tiny frame ready to rumble. Squeak trailed a little distance behind, throwing uncertain glances my way.

An older man sat in the Barks section, sipping his coffee. He waved a gnarled finger at Coal and the pups. "Seems an unfair fight," he said.

I took offense. "My Great Dane would never hurt them."

He smiled. "I meant those little whippersnappers are going to pounce your big dog—you mark my words. They look innocent, but trust me, Chihuahuas can be maniacs."

"You've had them?" I asked.

He nodded. "My wife had several through the years." He cleared his throat and worked his jaw. "She had one when she passed—Dynamite, her name was. She was a little stick of TNT, all right. But when she lost her person, she seemed to lose her will to live. Died the year after."

What an opportune thing that he'd chosen to visit the cafe when we had Chihuahua mixes in the house. Or maybe it was more than just a coincidence. Maybe it was a meant-to-be match.

I gestured to Pip and Squeak, who had planted themselves on Coal's exposed stomach, giving him occasional friendly nips. "Ever think of adopting another pup? Or maybe even two?"

He returned his watery stare to the dogs. "I'm afraid I'm too old to deal with that level of energy, especially times two." A thoughtful look crossed his face. "However...I do have a daughter who lives right next door. She's been looking for a puppy for my granddaughter." He tapped at his phone that was sitting on the table. "Maybe I should give her a call, see if she wants to drop in. Am I right in thinking you only keep the dogs here for one day, then return them to the shelter?"

"Usually," I said. "But if your daughter can't make it today, I can always ask if the shelter can hold them until she can get over there."

Fresh light sparked in his eyes. I'd seen that look many times in the cafe. It was the light of future memories waiting to be made. The light of hope.

"That would be much appreciated," he said. He picked up his phone. "I'm going to call her now."

BY THE TIME I got Coal home, I could tell he was exhausted. When I opened the garden gate, he trudged inside as if it would take a monumental effort to use the bathroom. I wouldn't throw him in with another puppy pack anytime soon.

Waffles, the dog next door, gave a few spastic barks, alerting us that she knew we were home. Coal ignored her, which was completely out of character, since the two loved to antagonize each other every chance they got.

My neighbor Vera called out to me, and I realized she was sitting out on her front porch, a favorite pastime of hers. I didn't blame her, because her porch was like a room unto itself, enclosed with low-hanging evergreen boughs that kept it cool. She motioned me over, so I made my way to one of her white wicker rockers, with no help from Waffles, who seemed intent on tripping me up by swirling around my legs.

Vera laughed as her rambunctious golden Labradoodle plopped down on top of my feet. "She's glad to have company, and so am I. You want a glass of sweet tea, hon?" She was already reaching for the pitcher that sat handy.

"Sure." Vera's sweet tea was not to be missed, especially as the days warmed up.

She poured it and handed me a glass, tilting her head to the side. Her short gray hair always lent her a spritely air, although her large brown eyes acted as a grounding force. She fixed me with an intense gaze. "The garden club's been buzzing about that actor's death. They said you and Bo found him in the hostas— is that right?"

I took a long sip, trying to ignore Waffles' body weight on my feet. "I noticed his shoes, then called Bo over. He kept people away and got hold of Charlie Hatcher."

"Very sensible," she affirmed. "Lawsie, to hear Matilda talk, you'd have thought she was right next to the dead body instead of working at the nearby Green home. Abigail said she had to remind her that she wasn't there."

I subtly shifted my feet, causing Waffles to rise into a sitting position. Unfortunately, this caused the bulk of her weight to press into the top of my right shoe. She gave me a happy look and wagged her tail, as if to say, "Isn't it wonderful we can be together again?"

Given all the adventures I'd had with the wayward rescue dog, I knew better than to fall for her innocent act. It was nothing short of a miracle that she behaved for Vera.

As pressure built on my foot, I gently shook her off, so I could refocus on the conversation at hand. "So you're close with Abigail?" I asked.

Vera took a drink. "I wouldn't say *close* close—more like casual friends. I joined the garden club the first year I came back, but I wound up getting more involved in my book club. This spring, I dropped out of garden club." She chuckled. "I really didn't want to have to volunteer for the home and garden tour. It's hours of sitting and making small talk, and I don't really care for that."

No. Vera wasn't a small talk kind of person. She knew how to cut to the heart of the matter, which I always found refreshing. Book club was a better venue for her. But I was having a sudden brainstorm.

"What does it take to get into the garden club?" I asked. "You know I love flowers, so maybe I should check into it."

She looked dubious. "There aren't any young people in there."

I smiled. "Vera, I'm forty now, remember?"

"Still young." She gave a brisk rap on the arm of her rocker. "Let me see. Matilda's in charge of meetings, so you could ask her if you could visit the next one and see what it's all about."

Talking to Matilda was hardly my idea of fun, but I thanked Vera and assured her I would. As soon as possible, in fact, because I'd promised Aspen I'd look into any connections Cody had in town. The garden club ladies had been on the spot, and they might've seen something that didn't register as important at the time.

It couldn't hurt to infiltrate their ranks and ask them a few questions.

BEFORE CALLING MATILDA, I tried to fortify myself with a quick snack of leftover beef on a roll. Coal had sagged on his pillow in the living room, and he didn't even watch as I ate. Once I felt reasonably restored, I picked up my phone and called Matilda.

"Hello?" she said loudly.

"Hi, Matilda; it's Macy Hatfield."

"Eh? Who's that again? Don't mumble now."

I recalled that Matilda eschewed cell phones—or "mobiles," as she called them. She must be on her land line at home. Either she needed a hearing aid, or her phone volume wasn't turned up enough.

"*Macy Hatfield*," I repeated, so forcefully that Coal's ears twitched, as if I'd offended him.

"Macy. Whatever could you want at this hour?"

The hour was only six o'clock, but I should've guessed Matilda went to bed early. "I'm sorry to bother you, but Vera said you'd be the person to talk to." A little ego-boosting might warm her up to my real reason for calling.

Her tone brightened. "Go on, then."

I explained that I was interested in joining the illustrious garden club and that I'd like to visit their next meeting.

Skepticism laced her English accent. "But do you know your onions about gardening?"

I had no idea what *knowing my onions* meant, but I quickly assured her I did. "I have plenty of flowerbeds that I putter around in all the time. Not that I wanted to be on the home tour next year or anything—after all, everyone knows the front of my house is the Barks & Beans Cafe." I gave a wobbly laugh.

Matilda remained silent, as if waiting to be convinced.

"You might recall that my great-aunt Athaleen planted all these flowerbeds," I added. "They're filled with her prizewinning roses, irises, tulips, and more. I've kept them up and added more bulbs each year." Somewhat grudgingly, I offered, "The club members would be welcome to drop by."

Ignoring my offer, she said, "Your aunt planted them, you say. Now if that just isn't the bee's knees." Something had shifted in our conversation, something I couldn't put my finger on, but it felt like I suddenly had the upper hand. Was it possible that Auntie A's name had triggered some kind of respect in the pompous Matilda Crump?

"I'll speak to Abigail Belcher, our club president," she said. "Keep those beds up, just in case." She hung up abruptly.

I stared at my phone. What was that supposed to mean?

Coal roused and gave me a sleepy look. "Yeah. I know," I said aloud. "What do I make of that? Is she saying they're going to randomly drop by my garden?" I considered the state of my flowerbeds. My peonies were still blooming, but my irises had already come and gone. I'd noticed some grass springing up here and there in my dirt.

I jumped to my feet, and Coal clambered into a standing position, ready to support me. "I have to get busy," I explained.

Once I'd changed into my well-worn gardening jeans and tee, I donned gloves and hurried outside. Coal lugged himself down the steps, then sat in the shade as I grabbed my clippers and hand trowel from the gardening shed.

Since Matilda only lived one street away, I wouldn't put it past her to change up her bedtime routine and stroll over to examine my flowers. I launched into trimming and weeding with a fury.

Later, Bo stopped by on his nightly jog. "You need anything for supper, sis?"

I wiped sweat from my forehead and glanced at my phone. "Oh, mercy, it's already seven thirty. These longer days are throwing me off, I guess." I considered his offer. "I am a little hungry. Do you have extra food?"

"Of course. It's hard to cook for just one. I'll finish this loop, then I'll drop off some barbeque beef sliders and potato wedges I made."

"That sounds great. Thanks, bro."

He jogged off, quickly speeding up to a pace I could never hope to keep up with. Running was his feel-good place, while lounging on the couch with a book or TV show was mine. I liked to think we evened each other out.

By the time I'd showered and eaten, Coal had uncharacteristically fallen asleep on the living room pillow. I knew he'd rouse to go upstairs with me when I headed up, but for now, I wanted him to rest, so I flipped on the TV.

A text came through from Aspen, who shared that she'd spent a lot of time wandering the well-kept grounds of Donovan Place. Her walk had cleared her head, she said.

I didn't share that I'd stumbled onto a dead woman lying in the fountain on those very grounds this past fall. I was hoping Milo's family had laid all those ghosts to rest when they'd bought and revamped the place.

Instead, I texted back that I was looking into people in town, and I asked if the police had given her any updates on her brother's death.

She texted that they hadn't, but that she would update me if she heard anything.

Soon after we finished texting, Titan called. I sat back and enjoyed the rich tones of his deep voice as he shared about his recent trip to a large city he wasn't at liberty to name specifically. This was part and parcel of his FBI job, and I knew better than to probe for details.

He was explaining how he'd visited a Vietnamese restaurant in the city and ordered noodle soup, or *pho*. "It had a really unusual taste with my first bite, but I kept eating," he said. "It was only afterward that my partner told me it had cow's stomach lining in it, better known as tripe." He chuckled. "Turns out, I actually like tripe."

"Good to know," I said. "Though I probably won't be cooking it up for you anytime soon." I stretched my legs out and pulled my couch blanket tighter, since the night was turning chilly. "Hey, would you happen to know anything about a bald guy with an anchor tattoo who used to sell drugs in these parts? I think he was known as 'Boss Hogg.'"

His voice took on a wary edge. "And why would you be asking me this? Bo would have the best information, given his DEA access."

"Bo keeps busy as the mayor," I said vaguely. My brother didn't need to know I was nosing around. Of course I didn't plan to *confront* Boss Hogg, just to check out his possible connection to Cody, but Bo wouldn't approve.

"Mm-*hmm*," Titan said knowingly. "I can look into it, but that doesn't mean I'm going to point you to the guy. With a name like Boss Hogg, he can't be good. He might even have connections with Leo Moreau or his wife."

Leo was a criminal mastermind my brother had finally helped put behind bars, thanks in large part to a tip-off from Leo's wife, Anne Louise. But, to no one's great surprise, Anne Louise had conveniently disappeared the moment her husband was imprisoned. Soon after, it became clear that she'd taken control of Leo's vast crime network, which had a firm grip in our home state.

"I know," I said. "But any information on his dealings in Lewisburg might be helpful...like big-picture stuff Detective Hatcher might not have time to follow up on."

"Big-picture," he repeated. "I see. I'll let you know if I run into anything interesting." His voice softened. "Have a good night, Macy."

Something about the way he said my name went beyond a glib term of endearment. It was heavy with all the words he knew better than to speak at this juncture in our relationship, since I was still easing into the idea that someone could love me for me. But it felt like he was protectively pulling me into the kind of hug I never wanted to extricate myself from. A hug filled with family, acceptance, and real, never-failing love.

"Good night," I whispered back.

8

I woke when the sound of the doorbell launched Coal into a furious spasm of barking. I groaned and flipped my phone over, only to see that it was six twenty. On my day off.

By the time I dragged myself out from under my quilt and threw on a robe, Coal was already downstairs, worked up into a regular frenzy. I muttered to myself, inwardly blasting the delivery driver who would stop by this time in the morning. I'd already asked them to leave packages on the porch without pressing the doorbell, because that sound drove Coal crazy. Everyone in my inner circle knew to knock instead of ring the bell.

I peeked out the side window, then quickly recoiled. Matilda Crump had chosen this time of day to drop by.

After vigorously shushing Coal, I pulled my robe tighter, opened the door, and attempted to smile.

Matilda gave me a disapproving once-over. "Oh, dear. I'd assumed you would be up by now, given that you have a job."

"It's my day off." I tightened my lips, trying to bite back a not-so-nice retort. Coal gave a barely perceptible growl, doubtless picking up on my mood.

Matilda peered at me through her glasses, leaning in closer on her cane. "I took the opportunity on my morning constitutional to examine your flowerbeds." She shot Coal a forbidding look as he took a step toward her. "I must say that I was surprised to see how tidy they are—possibly tidier than when Athaleen kept them."

I could see there'd been no love lost between Matilda and my great-aunt, but I had no idea why. "Um —okay. That's great. I'm glad you liked them," I said.

"The club would approve," she said briskly. "I plan to inform Abigail of your interest. In addition, the club will be meeting this afternoon to evaluate our home tour. We look for ways to improve it every year. Since it's your day off, you might want to attend. It will be conducted at my house at three in the afternoon, and there will be refreshments." She threw a black look at Coal. "No pets allowed, of course."

"Oh, of course—"

"Indeed." She gave me a parting nod, circling around toward the steps. "Cheerio for now."

I closed the door and crouched down to pet Coal. "I know she's not nice," I murmured. "But you have to be the bigger person."

He gave me a contrite look, so I grabbed a conciliatory doggie treat and handed it to him. In reality, my warning was as much for myself as it was for him. I needed to respond with kindness to Matilda, even though she perpetually rubbed me the wrong way. Not just to get in good with the garden club, but because something kept telling me that despite her prickly exterior, she was, at heart, a lonely widow with no one who truly cared for her.

I chuckled, thinking of the kind of foods Matilda might offer at her home. Stale oatmeal cream pies? Coffee that had been sitting on the burner for hours? Grapes with seeds in them? Regardless, I couldn't imagine she'd serve a treat for the taste buds.

I decided that since I was up, I might as well keep rolling. Maybe I'd do something fun before the club meeting this afternoon. I'd been eyeing a recently-opened bookstore that sat a couple of blocks over from Barks & Beans, so a visit seemed in order. The store was called Recycled Reads, and Kylie had told me it was well-stocked with used books.

After pulling up its website online, I found that it opened at ten. That gave me plenty of time to relax with coffee and breakfast before I headed out.

While I was keeping my mission for Aspen in mind, I could only cover so much ground each day. I'd poke around in the garden club this afternoon, but I couldn't exactly track down Boss Hogg, since I knew nothing of his connections or the places he might hole up. I had no real leads on Cody's murder, save the blonde lady in the back garden, and her description could fit any number of women around here.

Coal did a big stretch and gave a low groan, as if he'd spent all his energy this morning.

I patted the side of his soft jowl. "Guess what, boy? You're going to have a leisurely day at home." I headed into the kitchen, pulling out my bag of coffee beans and my French press. "And I'm going to enjoy this summer day in downtown Lewisburg."

THE SIGN that hung outside Recycled Reads had been artfully crafted with discarded metal objects. I pushed open the door and glanced around as a cloying, smoky scent assailed my nostrils. It didn't take long to realize a stick of incense was burning on the brightly colored checkout counter, which had been designed from thousands of bottle caps.

Whoever ran this place must have a serious creative streak, but there was no one around. After glancing at the bookshelf signs, I made my way toward the suspense section, figuring I'd check for Mary Higgins Clark books I didn't own yet.

I was deep into rereading the chilling book description for *Where are the Children?* when I sensed movement on my left. I turned and gave a jolt, because a man in his mid-forties had managed to sidle up right next to me.

"I'm sorry to startle you." He gave me a slow smile. "I didn't get to welcome you when you came in. I'm Arlo Edwards, the owner."

I was unable to piece together a coherent response in light of his dead-silent approach. "Thanks," I managed, trying not to stare.

Arlo looked like he'd time-traveled straight out of the hippie movement, with his long blond hair and beard, ragged jeans, and Birkenstocks. Yet his gray eyes were intelligent, and his breath smelled like coffee, which couldn't help but endear him to me.

I patted the book in my hand. "I was checking out your suspense section. You have a good selection."

He glanced at the title. "I like to keep plenty of our bestsellers stocked."

"I'm Macy Hatfield," I added. "My brother and I run the Barks & Beans Cafe."

A grin cracked his lips. "You're practically royalty in this town, then—supplying java for those who need it most. It's an honor to meet you, Miss Hatfield."

The door opened, and he glanced over his shoulder. "I'd better greet my new visitor. Have a mellow time looking through the shelves."

Immediately, the tune from "Mellow Yellow" played in my head, and I tried not to snicker. Arlo seemed to be stuck in the Sixties.

I pulled out a more recent psychological thriller and was flipping through the pages when I heard a familiar voice. Peeking around the bookshelf, I saw that Tobias had come in and was chatting with Arlo.

It struck me how cheery Tobias' tone was, almost as if his star client hadn't just been murdered. "I doubt you'd have it," he was saying. "But I thought I'd check."

Arlo walked over to his laptop that was sitting on the bottle-cap counter. "What's the title again? I'll check my inventory."

"I'm not sure. It would have *Wife of Poseidon* some-where in the title, I believe. It's a coffee table-type book picturing the actors who played in the movie. I'd guess it was published around 1999, when the film released."

A couple of moments later, Arlo gave a satisfied

smirk and pointed to his computer screen. "You're in luck. I recently ordered a copy, but it was never picked up. I'll show you to the nonfiction section."

As Arlo led Tobias into a side room, I decided on a couple of books that I wanted to buy. I headed to the counter, waiting a few minutes for the men to emerge. Sure enough, Tobias came out first, gripping an over-sized book in both hands. His eyes met mine and flickered with recognition.

He pointed at me. "You're from the dog cafe, right?"

I nodded. "I'm Macy. And I heard that you were Cody Franklin's manager—I'm so sorry."

"News travels fast in a small town, I guess." He gave me a flippant smile, which repelled me. This was his star client we were talking about—a client most managers would've killed to represent. And now he was dead.

Arlo seemed to be weighing the dynamic between the two of us. Taking my books to ring them up, he murmured, "Quite a tragedy."

Tobias managed to say, "Yes, it was," but then he checked his watch.

I looked at the cover of his book, which was titled *A Selection of Stills from Wife of Poseidon*. "A favorite movie of yours?" I asked.

He shook his head. "It's actually a movie Cody's mother starred in over twenty years ago. It was the last film she made before she died young of a heart attack. Cody was only four at the time. I knew he'd been looking for a copy of it, so I'm glad I found this here. I figured it'd be nice to display it at his memorial service back in California—once these bumpkin cops clear me to leave, that is."

Snarky responses weren't my forte, so I couldn't think of a quick retort to his derogatory comment. I glanced at Arlo, wondering if he'd say something, but he'd only just moved here from who knows where. Maybe he also felt the locals were bumpkins.

But, to his credit, Arlo raised a light eyebrow and leveled a very non-mellow gaze on Tobias. "Well, that's offensive," he said.

Tobias shrugged. "I'm just speaking the truth. They keep telling me autopsies can take months here. That's ridiculous. Show business can't wait around for those kinds of delays. If I have to hire a lawyer to get back to work, I will."

I took my bag from Arlo, shooting him a smile of solidarity. Tobias was stepping toward the counter before I'd even evacuated my position.

"Thanks," I said to Arlo. "I'll be sure to tell my friends about this place." I gave Tobias a tight smile. "I hope you can get out of here soon."

I strode out the door, wishing I could've come up with something to prove that West Virginia was a wonderful place to live. But I'd been around long enough to know that people like Tobias—and my ex-husband Jake—would only see the worst in my home state. They preferred to stew in their aggressive ignorance.

It was some comfort to me that Cody—a Holly-wood star—had chosen to move here. Granted, he might've had an underhanded motive, like making a connection with a drug dealer, but then again, maybe he'd simply craved peace and found our town a welcome respite.

I wanted to dig to the truth, for Aspen's sake. That way, she could say goodbye to her brother having a better picture of who he actually was. Although it seemed unlikely, it was still possible he'd told her the truth and cleaned up his life. Maybe the appearance of Boss Hogg on the home tour was just a fluke.

I crunched the paper book bag under my arm so I could open my back gate. Hopefully, I'd get some helpful perspective from the garden club ladies this afternoon.

9

I dove into one of my new books while eating a turkey sandwich for lunch. Once I'd finished a chapter and polished off my food, I reluctantly headed upstairs and changed into a black and white blouse and dark jeans.

I dabbed on some watermelon lipstick, donned my strappy black sandals, and took a deep breath. Hopefully, I was adequately prepared to join the ranks of Lewisburg's gardening elite.

Since the day was still mild, I decided to walk to Matilda's. As I approached her white two-story house, I took a closer look at her flowers, which weren't too impressive. Red knockout roses sprawled near the sidewalk, and unkempt hydrangea bushes framed her porch. She clearly didn't spend much time trimming, although her reliance on her cane probably made gardening difficult. I felt a twinge of pity for the formidable faux-Brit.

As I walked up the porch steps, I had to grin when I

saw a pair of binoculars sitting on an outdoor table. At least Matilda wasn't idle, even if she spent an inordinate amount of time spying on her neighbors.

I rang the doorbell, and it only took a moment for Matilda to appear. She must've been watching for me out the window. She wore a garishly bright geometric-print dress and heavy, thick-soled shoes.

"Good afternoon. We're glad you were able to join us today, Macy." She ushered me inside, adjusting her cane as she stepped from the tiles onto the nubby tan carpet. "Help yourself to some snacks in the kitchen. I don't think the queue is too long."

Not for the first time, I felt a sense of claustrophobia as I glanced around Matilda's dreary living room. Dark floral couches had been adorned with fringed, pastel pillows. Multiple china cabinets lined the walls, stuffed with British knickknacks, and teapots dotted nearly every open surface.

Trying not to topple anything, I greeted Opal, who was sitting near the couch, breaking a piece off a dry-looking pastry. "We're delighted to have you," she said.

Matilda settled into a chair, so I continued toward the kitchen, where I got stuck behind a "queue" of exactly two people. Abigail Belcher was standing behind a man with a heaped-up plate, and she turned to me and smiled. "We're so glad you could come."

"I am, too." I took a plate and scanned the food offerings on the kitchen counter, which were mostly lackluster. But when I saw the row of neatly-lined desserts, I gasped. "Oh, wow. I haven't had banana pudding in years."

Abigail spooned out a scoop of broccoli salad. "That's my mother's recipe," she said.

The man turned. He was younger than I expected, and solidly built. "Best banana pudding in these parts," he said.

"Trifle!" Matilda corrected, clomping up behind me. "It's properly called a trifle."

Abigail dipped her head. The man gave a little cough, grabbing a water bottle before moving into the living room.

Matilda gestured after him. "That's Jason Lilly. He's a landscaper with Lilly Designs."

"He owns the business, dear," Abigail said quietly.

"Of course he does." Matilda dumped several scoops of fruit cocktail into her small bowl. "I never said he didn't."

Abigail moved into the living room, so I followed her to the couch. I took the only remaining spot, next to Jason.

He shot me an understanding smile, as if he'd overheard the conversation with Matilda. He had kind eyes, and I was guessing he was in his thirties. "I'm Jason Lilly," he said. "Though you already know that. I'm pleased to meet you, Macy. You and Bo did a great job with the cafe renovation. It's really bringing tourists into the town."

"Thank you," I said, pleased at his praise. "But Bo handled all of it, really."

Matilda made her way toward her chair, somehow balancing her fruit cocktail bowl in one hand while gripping her cane with the other. After placing her bowl in a precarious position on the side table, she announced, "This is all of us, Opal. You can commence reading the minutes from our last meeting."

Opal duly commenced. I phased out as she went over the club's business, which didn't really interest me. I'd hoped the club meeting would provide practical gardening tips, but it seemed more geared toward town projects.

I was finishing my last bite of pudding when the topic shifted to the home and garden tour, so I tuned back in.

"The memorial shade garden in Mr. Franklin's back yard drew both history seekers and flower lovers during our tour," Opal reported.

"Not to mention a murderer," Matilda said drily.

Opal gave a few rapid blinks at that remark, and Jason took the opportunity to seize the floor.

"There wouldn't have *been* a memorial shade garden if *Mr. Franklin* had anything to do with it," he said. "Let's just be real. He didn't even want to acknowledge the presence of a Confederate soldier's bones on his property." Turning to me, he explained, "I did some genealogy research and discovered that I'm actually related to the soldier they found. I'm the one who lobbied to have a shade garden made in his honor. But Cody-boy was in the process of buying the place, and he threw a big stink that he didn't want that 'Reb soldier' recognized."

Abigail held out a calming hand. "Now, that's all behind us. Mr. Franklin finally agreed that we could design a tasteful bed and a memorial plaque."

"I designed it myself," Jason said proudly. His lips

twisted. "But it still doesn't change the fact that Cody didn't respect our Confederate heritage."

I gave a supportive nod, even though one of my own ancestors was shot for being a Yankee sympathizer. As a Hatfield, I'd learned long ago that nothing good came from bringing up old rifts. But, due to the Union takeover of Lewisburg in the Civil War, you could still dig up plenty of hard feelings if you went looking for them. I recalled how Abigail herself had said she had Confederate relatives, even though she was doing her best to keep things calm.

Matilda put on her best British accent. "I don't understand why there's always so much infighting here in the colonies."

Unable to hold back, I gave a loud snort. Jason covered his mouth with a napkin, trying to stop his own chortling.

Opal reined things in, launching into a detailed report of the tour's financial success. By the time the meeting concluded, I was pleasantly full of banana pudding—nay, *trifle*—and Jason had given me tips as to the best places to find mulch for my garden beds.

But as I was about to head home, Jason sidled up to me on the porch. In a low voice, he said, "To tell you the truth, I heard from a reliable source that Cody planned to renege on his promise and remove the memorial plaque. He even said he might vandalize it, then say it was too pricey to design a new memorial. That would've been a low blow, if you ask me."

It was a treacherous way to behave, that was for certain. As I said goodbye to Jason, I had to admit there was a possibility that Cody's destructive garden plans might have spurred the otherwise mild-mannered landscaper into taking action. The idea was far-fetched, but family ties ran deep, especially here in the mountains. Insulting someone's family was kicking a hornet's nest.

Still, Jason seemed levelheaded and helpful—not the sort of man who could shoot someone in the chest.

I wondered who Jason's "reliable source" was. From all reports, Cody hadn't been close to anyone in town. It didn't make sense that he'd be discussing a sabotage mission with anyone around here. Unless someone had overheard him talking about it, possibly on the phone.

Regardless of who'd been on the receiving end of Cody's vandalism discussion and who'd merely been eavesdropping, I needed something far more solid to share with Aspen in regard to who might have wanted her brother dead.

And while Cody had most likely been targeted for reasons that didn't involve his sister, I couldn't be certain of that fact. She was right to feel uneasy—I would, too, if I were in her shoes. I'd be ready to hightail it out of town.

10

Later that evening, I fixed myself a glass of iced decaf coffee, to which I added a liberal shot of brown sugar cinnamon syrup. Then I let Coal out the back door, grabbed my new Mary Higgins Clark book, and headed onto my porch. It was restorative when the late afternoon light dappled the grass and gardens, lending everything a magical glow.

Bo dropped by on his way home. He was wearing a close-fitting, charcoal gray tee that exposed some of his Marine tattoos. Summer and I joked that every time Bo's tattoos—and accordingly, his muscles—were out in the open, the cafe was suddenly flooded with women of all ages. Although Bo was largely unaware of his powers of attraction, Summer had told me she couldn't wait to stake her claim and get a wedding band on his finger.

Coal loped up to Bo's side and sat, politely waiting for a scrap of his attention.

Bo dropped a hand to Coal's head. "Hey, sis.

Summer told me those Chihuahua pups got placed today. Nice job."

"Oh, I'm glad to hear that! That man's daughter must've been able to adopt them both. What a great outcome."

"You have a talent for saying just the right thing in just the right way to convince people they need a dog." The admiration in my brother's voice touched me. "I was right to build the Barks section into our cafe. I know you thought it was a cuckoo idea at first, but—"

"It didn't take long to win me over," I finished. "You got me away from my ex and back home to West Virginia—right where I belong. I can never thank you enough."

He smiled. "It was a selfish move. I knew I couldn't run the cafe alone. Besides, you're better at dealing with the bills than I am."

Coal darted off after a mourning dove that had dared to settle on one of my flowerbeds. I leaned forward in my chair. "Have you gotten any updates on Cody's death yet?"

"As a matter of fact, I was coming over to tell you that Charlie said that in the preliminary post-mortem, a bullet from a .22 revolver was retrieved from Cody's chest. It had passed through part of his heart, but not through an artery, so that might explain the minimal bleeding. And it could have taken him up to five minutes to die, they said."

"So it's possible he wasn't even shot in the shade garden," I observed.

"Exactly. There are no official results yet—the official autopsy might take months, given our state's backlog. But it's enough for Charlie to run with for now. I'm sure they'll be doing tests on what's left of that bullet."

"And what about Boss Hogg?" I asked. "Has Charlie tracked him down?"

"No luck there," Bo said. "But we feel reasonably certain he was on the property that day. I'm sure they'll be doing toxicology testing on Cody, to see if he was using."

I sighed. "It'll crush his sister if he was."

Bo's eyes narrowed. "You know his sister?"

Two seconds too late, I realized my misstep. "Uh, yeah. She came to the Barks section the other day. Seemed really nice."

"And you just struck up a casual conversation with her about her brother's possible drug use?" His eyes blazed a brighter shade of blue. "I don't want you sniffing around anywhere *near* Boss Hogg, sis."

Coal had returned to the porch, and he gave a lonesome whine, as if he, too, didn't approve of my investigation. I gave him a reassuring head pat. "I'm not doing anything stupid."

"Okay," Bo said, but the dubious look on his face told me he was clearly unconvinced.

As NIGHT FELL, I got restless reading my book. It occurred to me that I could try to find the *Wife of Poseidon* movie that Cody's mom had acted in. After checking for it on multiple streaming channels, I finally found one that had it, even though it cost $3.99 to rent it.

The title font and music were very late 90s, as were the women's over-plucked eyebrows and blown-out straight hair. When Cody's mom stepped on screen as Amphitrite, goddess of the sea and intended wife of Poseidon, I was surprised at how much she contrasted with Aspen. Where Aspen was tall and willowy, Wendy Franklin was petite and curvy. Where Aspen had light eyes and hair, Wendy's eyes and hair were dark as night. I could see some resemblance in her smile and eyes to Cody, but I saw no similarities with Aspen. Genetics were a tricky thing.

Wendy was positively effervescent, and I could see how Cody had inherited his mother's ability to appear natural on the screen. Her character had several memorable scenes, including one where she ran off a cliff and dove into the ocean, and one where she swam with sharks, both of which made me hold my breath. Of course, she probably hadn't performed such dangerous stunts herself.

Intrigued by Wendy's tragic early death, I looked her up online. Apparently, she'd died the next year, soon after the movie released. Her husband, who was father to their four-year-old boy, swore he would never marry again. But, lo and behold, the next year, he did remarry—and this time, to a Swiss supermodel named Leni. Together, they had Aspen, which explained why she didn't resemble Wendy in the least.

As the movie came to a close, I couldn't stop marveling at Wendy's hypnotic screen presence. Poseidon himself seemed to have more than a little chemistry with her, given the intensity of their kissing scenes. Cody had received a healthy dose of his mother's magnetism, which had doubtless jettisoned him toward fame.

I wondered if Aspen would be as successful in her acting career, which, according to Summer's online entertainment sources, was poised to launch soon. I'd have to ask her about it.

ASPEN SHOWED up at the cafe around eleven on Wednesday, during a lull. She asked Milo for a cappuccino and a pesto-stuffed baguette to go, then she grabbed her order and made a beeline for the Barks section.

She glanced at the dogs of the day. We had a mostly white dog named Corolla and a black and white pit bull mix named Franco. Both were extremely shy, even with each other. They'd each chosen a corner of the play area and had stayed in their own zones all morning.

"You got the puppies placed?" she asked hopefully.

I assured her that we had, and she looked relieved. But her face quickly fell. "I haven't heard much from the police, except that I'm not released to leave yet. Same goes for Tobias, who can't stop griping about how little there is to do here." She gave me an apologetic look. "But I plan to make some fun for myself today. In fact, I was thinking of going over to that salt spa not far from here. Would you like to join me and catch me up on anything you've found out? It'll be my treat."

Those were the magic words. I maintained a tight budget, since I was paying off my new car and saving up to renovate my downstairs bathroom. While I was sure the spa treatments were worth every penny, I wasn't about to splash out for such a treat for myself. But since Aspen was willing to pay...

"Sure, I'd love to. I'll be finished at one thirty. You want me to pick you up at your inn?"

"Actually, I'll be going through things at Cody's house, so if you could pick me up there, that would be great. I do have a rental car, but these roads can be so curvy. I have zero confidence driving them."

She walked over to give each dog's head a pat, then returned to me. "Good luck with those two. I'll book our appointments for three, if that works?"

"Definitely. Thanks for asking me."

She smiled. "You're the only friend I have here. See you soon." Gripping her sandwich bag tighter, she went through the gate and headed out the door.

As I threw a toy to each reclusive dog, Aspen's words looped through my mind. If she really considered me her only friend here, what did that make Tobias?

11

As I pulled up to the curb outside Cody's house, I was disappointed to see that Chancellor had taken up two parking spaces with his oversized blue truck. I didn't want to have another run-in with the cocky contractor, so hopefully Aspen would answer when I knocked.

But as I drew closer to the house, I caught sight of Aspen and Chancellor standing on the front porch, deep in an argument.

Aspen flailed her hands. "I'm giving you two weeks to finish this job. Otherwise, I'll fire you and get someone else."

He gave a toss of his dark hair and chuckled. "Good luck. You won't get anyone around here who'll work half as fast as I do. Besides, your timeline is unrealistic. Every time I fix one thing, I turn up something else that's falling apart." With a condescending huff, he added, "That's the nature of old houses, like this one your brother *chose*, ma'am."

In our area, when people called you "ma'am," it was a term of politeness. But Chancellor was wielding the word like an insult, and Aspen wasn't about to have it.

"Two weeks. That's all I'm paying you for." She gave me a low wave. "I'll be right out." She stepped inside the front door, allowing Chancellor to turn all his unwanted attentions toward me.

I looked down and kicked at a pebble on the sidewalk, unwilling to get involved in this fight.

But Chancellor was already jogging my way. He didn't stop until he'd completely invaded my bubble of personal space. In a low, almost intimate tone, he said, "Macy, I wish you'd explain to that dragon-woman that complete house renovations take time. You know I'm the best contractor around. I can't understand why she's not getting that."

Aspen slammed the front door and charged down the steps, cradling a metal lamp in her hands. I forced myself to meet Chancellor's all-too-close brown eyes. "Maybe it's because you're not the best contractor around—at least when it comes to listening to your clients. It helps if you don't antagonize them."

His smug look shifted and his eyes flashed. "You'd do well to remember who you're talking to." He stalked away, forcefully brushing into Aspen's shoulder as he walked past her.

She shot him a glare before coming to a stop by my side, looking menacing with her battered, shadeless lamp.

"I'm sorry you had to see that," she said. "I really don't like confrontations, but I won't back down from one, either."

I opened my SUV passenger door, and she gratefully took a seat. As I got in the driver's side, she turned to place her lamp on the back floor. "I don't know why Cody kept this old thing," she said. "I think it was our dad's. I grabbed the first thing that came to hand, just in case. Sometimes Chancellor acts so erratic, I wonder if he's on something. Yesterday, he bought new pulls for my bathroom drawers without asking for an okay on them. The style was all wrong."

As I wheeled away from the curb, I considered the possibility that *Chancellor* might've been the one meeting with Boss Hogg on the day Cody died. That would throw a different light on things.

I glanced at Aspen, who was obviously still upset by her fight with Chancellor. Trying to put her mind at ease, I said, "I'm sorry he acted so ugly toward you. And he's blowing smoke—there are plenty of contractors around who could handle your renovation." I leaned into her mention of her dad, since she'd brought it up. "I read that you and Cody were half-siblings?"

She pushed a strand of hair from her eyes. "That's right. Same dad, different moms. Cody's mom died really young. Our dad remarried and they had me soon after, so we basically grew up together. Dad died when I was in college." Tears welled up in her eyes and she tried to blink them away. "Cody used to make me peanut butter and banana sandwiches for school."

The tragedy of her brother's violent death was probably starting to hit home for her. I tried to steer toward a safer subject. Giving her a gentle smile, I asked, "What kind of treatment did you book today?"

She perked up a little. "I booked us both a tropical facial and a back massage. I hope that works for you?"

"Definitely." I was certain both services didn't come cheap, and I appreciated her generosity. "I can't wait."

ASPEN STAYED pensive the rest of our drive. But she brightened once the quaint spa came into sight, tucked into the green hillside like a hobbit house.

"Oh, how delightful," she breathed.

"They have a great little cafe, too. I'll cover our lunch there," I offered.

Her shoulders seemed to relax, and she gave me a meaningful smile. "I'd love that."

I led her up the flower-lined path to the spa's bright purple front door. Inside, the spacious welcome area was designed to look like a cave, with a vaulted stone ceiling. Products lined the wall shelves, and salt lights glowed from every nook and cranny.

Since we'd arrived early, the receptionist asked if we wanted to pay extra to relax in the salt cave room before our treatments. Aspen seemed enthused about the possibility, so I agreed.

We took the blankets, white socks, and eye masks the receptionist handed us. I pushed open the wooden doors, and we stepped into the cool, peach-lit room. Muted harp music piped overhead, and a water fountain had been set into one wall. A woman reclined in one of the black zero-gravity chairs, with a towel wrap on her head and an oversized velour mask over her eyes.

Aspen and I had agreed not to talk during our spa treatments so we wouldn't feel pressured to keep up conversation. She seemed to have the same idea for the salt cave, since she silently settled into a chair. After pulling on her socks, she draped the blanket around her body and closed her eyes.

Before getting comfortable, I glanced at the other lady again . Something about her seemed familiar, but I couldn't put my finger on it. Maybe she was a regular at the cafe?

I slipped on the mask, leaned back, and gave myself the chance to ruminate over what I'd learned about Cody's life and times during the past few days.

First, he'd been getting his house renovated by Chancellor, who'd made it sound like he didn't know Boss Hogg personally. But maybe he'd lied to me. Maybe *he* was the one Boss Hogg came to see during the garden tour, and maybe Cody had witnessed a drug transaction, making him a liability.

Then there was Tobias, who seemed completely unaffected by his star client's sudden death—almost unsurprised by it. And he already had a Plan B in place, since he'd struck some kind of deal with Aspen to act in a big movie. I'd need to find a tactful way to ask her about that.

But Tobias didn't seem the type to know how to handle a gun, much less have the wherewithal to shoot Cody at close range. Plus, he would've needed to transport his firearm on multiple plane trips and layovers from California to West Virginia and back again, which seemed impossible.

Jason from the garden club had a motive—though

hardly a deadly one—to get Cody out of the way. Maybe he'd gotten so worked up about the possibility the memorial would be destroyed, he'd decided to make sure it would stand by taking matters into his own hands. But that just didn't jibe with his personality.

When it came right down to it, I had no brilliant insights to offer Aspen. Although she was in regular contact with Chancellor and Tobias, I didn't believe either would have a motive to kill her. More like motives to work *with* her. I'd update her on what I'd learned, but we could only hope that Charlie was having more success with his homicide investigation than I was.

The other woman stirred. Being the innately curious person I was, I discreetly pushed my mask up to my forehead, so I could watch as she walked by and maybe place a name to her.

It took a few seconds for her to move my way. My breath caught as her mid-length, ice-blonde hair spilled over her shoulders. Now it made sense why I recognized her—she was the petite woman who'd been lurking in Cody's back yard when we found his body.

She was dressed in the "coastal grandmother" look, wearing wide-leg linen pants and a blue button-up shirt, and she carried a large straw tote. She wore several layered gold bracelets and multiple diamond rings. Her head swiveled ever so slightly in my direction, and I could make out that she had a sharp chin and tan cheeks that had been unnaturally plumped by fillers.

But when her eyes met and held mine, a jolt ran

down my spine. The look she gave me was as Arctic as her hair, and completely devoid of feeling. I had no idea what she was thinking about me, yet I could sense that she knew exactly who I was.

As she pushed through the wooden door, I patted Aspen's arm. "I'm going to run to the bathroom really quick," I said. Jumping to my feet, I hurried after the blonde, only to find she wasn't in the welcome area.

On the off-chance she *had* stopped by the bathroom, I hurried that way, pushing open the padded leather door. But both stalls were empty.

I headed back to the salt cave, feeling a strange certainty that our wordless encounter wouldn't be the last. The blonde had recognized me from the garden, and, given the way she'd vanished, she must've realized I was on a mission to figure out why she'd been lurking around a crime scene.

12

For our tropical facials, we draped ourselves in sheets and stretched out on parallel tables in a dimly lit room. My massage therapist wrapped a towel around my head, then pressed warm, folded wash-cloths along my face in repetitive strokes. As she worked her way through fruit-scented scrubs, oils, and lotions, I lost all train of thought and started to fall asleep.

My therapist had moved on to my back massage when my phone vibrated, jarring me back into the moment. As the buzzing continued, I realized it might be some kind of emergency, so I asked her to stop for a moment. She handed me a robe, then I eased off the table and made my way toward a darkened corner of the room.

Bo was on the other end. "I'm sorry to bother you, but something's come up. They found Tobias Blum dead in his bathroom at the General Lewis this morning—looks like a heroin overdose. Charlie's having me check into any previous drug records. I just wanted to let you know. You at home?"

I hadn't exactly told Bo where I was going this afternoon, and I wasn't sure I wanted to tell him. But he seemed to read my silence like a book.

"You're hanging out with Aspen, aren't you? Milo mentioned that some tall blonde with a Chanel bag stopped by and talked with you. I couldn't think of any of your friends that fit that description."

Now my barista was spying on me, however unwittingly. But I wasn't going to apologize for trying to help a grieving sister. Keeping my voice low as Aspen's therapist continued her massage, I said, "That's right. She asked me to go to the salt spa with her, and I figured it would be good for her to get out."

"You'll need to let her know about Tobias, then, since Charlie will be touching base with her. She's the only person Tobias knew here." He hesitated. "And you might want to think about the implications of that fact, sis."

I didn't want to get into it here, but I thought his "implications" were way off. "I'll let her know," I said, trying to stay noncommittal. There's no way Aspen was mixed up in something nefarious with Tobias. She didn't even really like the man.

I said goodbye and headed toward my table, easing out of my robe before slipping under the sheet.

Aspen's voice was muffled as her therapist kneaded her lower back. "Everything okay?"

I didn't want to share about Tobias' death and ruin

the remainder of Aspen's spa experience. Since it seemed like our massages were winding to a close, I decided to wait until afterward, when we could talk about things at the spa cafe.

"I'll tell you soon," I said, settling my face into the padded head support.

But even as the therapist worked at the kinks in my shoulders, I felt like my entire body was tightening up instead of relaxing. I hated it when Bo forced me to stop and think, which was exactly what he'd done when he'd insinuated that Aspen might somehow be involved in Tobias' death.

But what earthly motive would she have? Anyway, Tobias had overdosed, which was likely his own doing.

Had I been off base to assume that Boss Hogg was Cody's dealer? What if Tobias was the one who'd been supplying his client with drugs?

Maybe Aspen was holding out on me. If she knew of Tobias' addiction, she might've decided to shield him from the police when her brother died.

And why wouldn't she? Tobias was her ticket to fame.

Aspen sipped at her lemon vanilla smoothie, blinking in what seemed like genuine disbelief. "You have *got* to be kidding me. I had no idea Tobias was into heroin." She frowned, obviously distressed.

I'd often wondered how those closest to addicts could miss the signs of drug use. Bo had explained that drug dependency didn't always show up in obvious ways, like tooth loss or extreme emaciation. Physically, addiction could show up as nothing more than a flushed face, runny nose, or bloodshot eyes. Emotional shifts like heightened elation, irritation, or tiredness could be explained away.

In short, if you weren't paying close attention—even if you were living with that person—you could miss it, at least up to a certain point. And Aspen had lived across the country from both Tobias and her brother.

I didn't want to ask my next question, but I forced myself to. "How did you know that your brother was on drugs? Did he tell you, or did you see him using?"

She fiddled with her salad fork. "His ex-wife Lizzie shared about his drug use two years ago, in their divorce proceedings. She claimed that's why she had to leave him. It was all over the news." She sighed. "I asked, and Tobias told me it was all true. He said that Cody liked to party with a dangerous bunch, and that he couldn't convince him to get away from them. I never personally saw Cody using, but he did ask me for money the year he divorced. I wasn't sure if it was because Lizzie had taken everything or because he wanted drugs." She stuck a lone piece of lettuce in her mouth and munched on it, looking totally dejected.

"Did you give him money?" I asked.

She shook her head. "Maybe I made the wrong decision, but I told him I didn't have anything to spare, which wasn't far from the truth. I told him to enroll in a real rehab—not some cushy movie-star one—and then pick up another movie job. It's not like he couldn't earn money honestly."

I nodded. "Right. That sounds wise. Did he go to rehab?"

"Tobias told me he did, even though it was just a three-month thing. Experts recommend a year for best results—believe me, I did my research. But Cody started calling me weekly once he got out, and we had some great conversations. He seemed to be back on track, so when he told me he was buying a place in West Virginia so he could have a quiet retreat, I encouraged him to go for it. I figured if he visited the East Coast more, I could get more involved in his life."

"Sounds like a positive move." I took a bite of my club sandwich, hoping she'd continue.

Her blue eyes rested on me. "I thought so. When I told him I wasn't exactly killing it carving out a folk music career in Nashville, he suggested that I apply for a lead role in an upcoming film. I didn't think I had a chance, but Cody sent my audition to Tobias, and he offered representation. When I got the role, Cody was so excited, he flew me here so we could talk about my future." She brought another fork-full of salad to her lips and chewed in silence.

I prodded a bit more. "So Tobias was your manager, too. To be honest, I didn't get the feeling you liked him much."

"He could be a jerk." Angry color flushed her cheeks. "Now I'm realizing maybe it was his drug use talking." She slammed her fork onto her bowl, causing the cashier to shoot an uneasy look our way.

But Aspen continued her tirade. "Tobias tattled on my brother, telling me he was hanging around dangerous druggies, yet there he was, every bit as involved." She flashed her teeth and gave a low growl, like she wanted to take a bite out of someone. "Who's to say he wasn't the one dealing to Cody all these years? Maybe the nefarious party gang was just a sham."

I had to hand it to Aspen—she was quite expressive when her emotions rose to the surface. And she'd clearly felt protective toward her brother, like I was.

I tried to redirect her thoughts. "You should probably go in and tell Detective Hatcher what you're thinking. He'll want to know about your dealings with Tobias."

"You're right." She jumped to her feet. "Would you mind dropping me at the station?"

The cashier still looked uneasy, so I gave her a calm smile as I stood. "I'd be happy to," I told Aspen, gathering my trash from the table.

As we walked to the car, anger radiated from Aspen in palpable waves. Tobias' death had sideswiped her, and not simply because she'd lost her manager. Tobias had probably been lying to her about her brother's unsavory connections in California, all the while supplying him with drugs himself.

Yet somehow, Cody had woken up to his desperate state and gone to rehab, no thanks to his drug-using manager. Had he truly come out clean?

I couldn't understand why a manager would push his biggest-name actor into something that would inevitably wreck his income stream, though. And if Cody had known Tobias was a dealer, why on earth would he have suggested his sister sign with him? Nothing was adding up.

I decided I'd have Bo over tonight and lay out the conflicting facts for him. Since he was no stranger to drug-related motivations, he'd likely have a good guess as to the real story behind Cody's baffling relationship with his manager.

13

Aspen texted me while I was pulling weeds, saying she'd had a good talk with Detective Hatcher and that an officer had driven her back to Donovan Place. She said she planned to order pizza and try to forget her worries by binge-watching old episodes of *Frasier*.

Bo accepted my invitation to come over, so I decided to contribute to the greater good by whipping up one of the handiest meals I knew how to make: buffalo chicken dip (made with canned chicken, of course), tortilla chips, and veggies. It was also one of my favorite meals. I wasn't sure if Bo felt the same, but he always ate quite a bit, then made sure to comment on how tasty it was.

After we'd eaten, we sat on the couch, where Coal pressed his large frame as close to Bo's leg as he possibly could. I decided to dive right in, so I gave Bo a rundown on our day—first, how Chancellor had such a punk attitude toward Aspen, then how I spotted the ice blonde from the garden tour in the spa, and finally, how Aspen's anger had flared toward her now-dead manager.

"Do you think Tobias was selling drugs to Cody? Have you heard anything about him in your DEA circles?" I asked.

Bo chuckled. "I'm not as active in my circles as I used to be. I did retire early, remember?"

I snorted. "I know you only have to ask, and information will be shared. Your friends are loyal to you."

He shifted his leg, probably so it wouldn't go to sleep with Coal's weight on it. Coal looked at him like he'd abandoned him on the roadside.

"I did look him up, sis. Tobias Blum has some previous record of heroin abuse, but it was maybe ten years ago. He actually went into rehab at that time. There's nothing recent on him."

"Maybe he relapsed," I said. "Though I don't know why. He was repping one of the biggest names in Hollywood, and he'd just signed the guy's sister for a big film."

Bo furrowed his red brows. "I know, but doesn't that bother you? Aspen had all her cards in place when her brother died. She was all set to blast off. You know Cody had to be worth a fortune, right? I'm wondering if she got his money."

I hadn't thought of that. Apparently, she'd gotten his house, because she was the one in charge of renovations now. She'd said her dad died when she was in college, so logically, Cody's estate would fall to her, his one remaining close relative.

I squeezed my couch pillow tighter. "I don't know. I haven't figured out a polite way to bring up the subject."

He nodded. "I know you're trying to help her out while she's stranded here, waiting for the police to clear her for home. But you need to keep in mind that Charlie can't rule her out as a suspect in Cody's death. And now, one of his other suspects is dead."

"Wait—are you hinting that Aspen could've had something to do with Tobias' death?" Realization began to dawn. "Were you at the scene?"

"I was. Charlie wanted me there since I've been at overdose scenes too many times to count. And I have to tell you, something was off. Sure, Tobias had needle tracks in his arm and he was lying on the bathroom floor with empty syringes next to him, but something didn't look right. I'm hoping the crime scene photos might show something I missed."

"It is strange that he hasn't used for years, then he suddenly started it up, just when things were going well for him." I pondered for a moment. "I suppose Cody's death could have thrown him into a bad spiral, but he didn't act all that bothered by it when I ran into him at the bookstore."

"Motives for drug use are far from logical," Bo said. "Sometimes it simply has to do with access."

A thought occurred to me. "Maybe he found the heroin at Cody's place, if he went over after he died."

Bo straightened. "Or maybe he found it *before.* Maybe he and Cody argued about it. Tobias might've threatened to take the drugs. If Cody got violent, it's possible Tobias could've shot him."

I shook my head. "I just can't see Tobias having a

gun. How would he have gotten it across the country on planes?"

"There are ways, but they seem too risky for someone in Tobias' position." He sighed. "They really need to find that murder weapon."

"Did they find anything suspicious in his room?"

"Nothing but the heroin. His rental car had nothing in it, either, save a big book they found behind a spare tire. We don't even know if it was his."

Recalling Tobias' bookstore purchase, I asked, "Did it happen to be a book about a movie?"

Bo gave me a curious look. "It was. How did you know that?"

"I saw him buy it at the bookstore. It was his book, all right." Recalling how Tobias had planned to display it at Cody's memorial service, I asked, "Do you think Charlie would release that book to Aspen, once it's been dusted for prints? It has Cody's mom in it, and it would be something special to include in his memorial —whenever they're able to do that."

"Sure, I'll text Charlie about that now." As Bo texted, Coal sneakily inched closer to his leg. By the time he put his phone down, Coal's head was resting on his knee. He smiled and gave Coal an ear rub. "You'll have to come over and see Stormy soon," he murmured.

At the mention of Stormy's name, Coal's head jerked up and he glanced around, as if he'd missed something.

"At Bo's house," I explained, pointing up the road. "She's not here."

"You're talking to your dog like he's human again," Bo said.

I raised my chin. "My boyfriend loves that I do that."

Bo snickered. "Does he, now? I'm going to have to tell Titan he's turned into a big softie."

I took a light swipe at his arm. "He won't care. Anyway, you talk to Stormy like she's human —admit it."

He considered for a moment. "Yeah, I do talk to her, but I don't *explain* things to her."

Feeling sassy, I retorted, "That's why she's not as smart as Coal."

Bo laughed. "I love ya, sis. I'd better get going so I can squeeze in a jog. Gotta stay in shape for my woman."

I gave an exaggerated roll of my eyes. "Yeah, because that's the only reason she's marrying you."

"It might be," he joked, grabbing his container of leftover buffalo dip and raising one arm. "I'll let you know if Charlie digs up anything new. And you know the drill—watch your back, so I don't have to."

I laughed, and Coal snuggled up next to me as Bo headed out. As I stroked Coal's back, I said, "If I didn't know better, I'd think you were fonder of my brother than of me."

He gave a whine and yawned, obviously nervous that he might have displeased me in some way. I leaned down and pressed my head to his. "Don't worry. I'm glad you love the people I love, my big boy."

Thursday morning went smoothly at the cafe. The shelter dogs were docile, and several customers seemed interested in adopting them. By the time I handed things over to Bristol, I was getting hungry for some of my buffalo dip.

Bo was approaching the cafe door just as I headed out, and he placed a book in my hands. "I got this from Charlie. He cleared it for you to give Aspen. The only prints on it were Tobias' and some partial prints they couldn't identify. I figure those belonged to the book-store owner—do you know his name?"

I thought for a moment. "Arlo...Edwards, I think he said. Unusual first name for an unusual guy. But he seemed nice, though. He actually stood up for me when Tobias was being rude."

Bo gave an approving nod. "Good for him. I'll get his name to the detective to make sure the prints were his. But they've been catalogued, so Aspen can take the book. It looks interesting."

I glanced down at the cover, which featured large center photos of Wendy Franklin and her co-star wearing Greek garb. Smaller photos framed the large ones, showing action scenes from the movie.

"The movie itself was actually quite good. I rented it the other night." I tucked the book under my arm. "Thanks, bro. I'll get it to Aspen."

As I rounded the sidewalk corner, a black truck with dark-tinted windows pulled out and started creeping along beside me, matching my slow pace. Music blared from its speakers, practically shaking the ground next to me.

Irritated, I glanced over. The passenger side window began to inch down, and I was able to make out a big man with a bald head. Suddenly feeling like a target, I turned and ran back toward the cafe, figuring the truck couldn't make a U-turn in the narrow road.

Bo hurried toward me the moment I burst in the door. When I breathily explained what had happened, he raced outside. I heard him shout, "Hey!" but by the time I looked around the corner, he was standing next to my back gate, peering up the block. The truck was nowhere in sight, so it must've whipped onto the connecting back road.

I walked toward my brother, feeling shaken. "I don't know what he wanted," I said. "But he was bald. And he was looking at me like he wanted to kill me. What if he was Boss Hogg?"

Bo's face was red, like he was ready to explode. "How *dare* he try to threaten you? What have you ever done to him? Did you get the plate number?"

I shook my head. "He was driving right alongside me. When I turned and ran, I didn't look back."

With his eyes glued to the street, Bo pulled me into a hug. "Of course you didn't. That was a smart move, turning back to the cafe."

I didn't have to explain that I'd known he'd come running to help me, carrying his trusty Glock in his belt holster.

Vera stepped onto the sidewalk, her face worried. "What's going on? I heard your shout, Bo." She looked at me. "Oh, honey, are you okay?"

Her affectionate use of the word "honey" reduced me to a sudden pool of tears. I stepped into her open arms and sobbed. She patted my head, saying "There, there," until I finally calmed down.

By now, Kylie and Jimmy had positioned themselves by the corner of the cafe. Kylie's jaw was set, and she had one combat boot forward, like she was ready to chase and tackle someone. Jimmy resembled the buses he used to drive—a thick, imposing wall of a man.

While it was heartening to know I always had a ready-made backup crew, I waved them back into the cafe. "It's okay. Everything's fine."

Yet I knew it wasn't. That bald truck driver was still out there, and whether or not he was Boss Hogg, he seemed to have some unfinished business with me.

14

O nce I'd calmed down and eaten a few chips and
dip, I gave Aspen a call.

"I have a coffee table book Tobias bought for your
brother's memorial service—it has photos of his mom's
Poseidon movie. You want me to drop it off?" A drive
into the countryside would get me out of my head,
since I couldn't stop thinking about the truck stalker.

"Actually, I'm in town right now. I'm at Cody's,
painting his kitchen. You want to swing by when you
get a chance?"

"You're painting? I thought that was part of Chancellor's job."

She groaned. "Not anymore. I fired him this morning. When I drove in, I caught him sitting in some guy's
truck. They had to be smoking weed, since the smell
was rolling out their open windows. He hadn't even
started work."

I had a wild hunch. "What color was the truck?"

"Black. Dark windows, huge tires, all the trappings

designed to intimidate. I don't know who the guy was, but he glared at me like he hated me."

"And let me guess—he was bald," I said.

"He was! How'd you know?"

I didn't feel like rehashing my earlier experience over the phone, though I'd have to fill her in on it sooner rather than later. If the bald man was Boss Hogg, Aspen needed to be aware that he was a drug dealer who might've had contact with her brother.

"Small town." I changed the subject. "Hey, would you like me to pick up a coffee for you?"

"I'd love that! Maybe an iced mocha latte? But no worries if you don't have time."

"I'll make time. I'll grab one for both of us, then head your way."

I DECIDED to take Coal along, just in case the bald guy decided to pay a repeat visit to Cody's house. I planned to tell Aspen to keep her distance if he showed up again, but to get his license number, if possible. That way, the police could start tracking him.

Coal seemed to sense my apprehension as I turned onto Cody's sidewalk, so he slowed down and plodded along next to me. Thankfully, there were no trucks in sight as I walked up to the porch and rang the doorbell.

Aspen greeted me wearing an oversized button-up men's shirt. Tiffany-blue paint streaked her perfect oval forehead, blonde hair, and shirt. The look was so incongruous—like Grace Kelly had joined in some kind of wild paint party—that I had to grin.

Extending the drink carrier, I said, "One iced mocha latte, coming right up."

She motioned me inside. "Come on into the living room. The kitchen's a mess right now."

We sat on a couple of mismatched 80s-era chairs that probably came with the house when Cody bought it. I set the *Wife of Poseidon* book on a side table so I could drink my coffee before sharing about it.

Aspen smiled at Coal, who had stretched out by the front door, where he'd placed himself on guard duty. "Brought your canine companion along, I see." In a higher tone, she spoke to Coal. "Aren't you a good boy?"

He thumped his tail on the floor and gave her a soft-eyed smile. I realized that one of the things holding me back from considering Aspen a serious suspect was the fact that my dog seemed to approve of her.

I told Aspen about the bald man in the truck—the way he'd stalked me and my suspicions that he was Boss Hogg—and she whistled. "I'd never seen him before today, but if he supplied drugs to my brother, I'm glad I fired Chancellor. I don't want anyone like that hanging around." She sighed and stood. "I'd better get back to work. I keep thinking the detective will call me soon and tell me I can fly out, so it's on me to finish this paint job. But I need a new contractor I can trust to finish this renovation, even if I leave the area."

"I know a guy who's reliable," I said. "He did a lot of work on the cafe. His name's Ash. I'll get his number for you." I stood. "And I'll help you paint. I'm off work for the day, and I don't have anything else I need to do."

She led me into the kitchen and gestured in a wide circle. "Are you sure? You don't have to stay. I still have to finish the ceiling and two full walls." She popped the lid off a paint can, stirred it, and poured it into the tray.

"I love how the color contrasts with your dark cabinets," I said. "And of course I'm sure. I wouldn't have offered otherwise."

She raised an eyebrow. "Macy, I swear you've been like some kind of angel to me. You keep that up and I'll be tempted to consider moving into my brother's house myself."

I was about to respond when I glanced out the window and saw a large man standing in the back yard, his back to us. Freezing in place, I pointed. "Who's that?"

She looked out. "I don't know," she said quietly.

Calling for Coal, I snapped his leash on and said, "I'll go check."

"I'm coming with you," Aspen said.

With Coal in the lead, we headed out the back door and toward the hosta bed, where the man was bent forward, reaching beneath the leaves.

Trying to think of what Bo might say in this situation, I used my boldest tone and blurted out, "Could we help you with something?"

He whirled around, and I realized it was Jason Lilly from the garden club. What was he doing trespassing in Aspen's yard?

"Oh, I'm sorry, ladies," he said politely. "The club has permission to care for the memorial bed as needed. I came over to trim some dead leaves—I hope you don't mind."

I glanced down. He was gripping pruning shears in one of his gloved hands, lending credence to his story.

Coal stared up at me, as if wondering what he was supposed to do next. "Sit," I commanded.

Aspen stepped in and spoke to Jason. "Sure, that's fine. I'm Aspen Franklin."

He blinked, probably recognizing her last name. "I'm sorry to intrude, especially after...well, I heard you were finished with renovations, so I assumed no one would be home."

Her lips flicked downward. "How'd you hear that?"

"Chancellor Huddnall—your contractor, I believe? He told me he was done working here."

"You're in close contact with Chancellor?" I asked. Was he actually friends with the exasperating contractor?

"We wind up working the same jobs, since he does building work and I do landscaping," Jason explained. He seemed to be trying to distance himself from Chancellor, which was a plus, in my estimation. "He was grabbing breakfast this morning at the same place I was, so I asked how things were going. He told me he'd finished the Franklin job."

"More like he got fired from it," Aspen said.

Jason held up his hands. "I don't even want to know. I'll still have to work with him." Glancing at his smartwatch, he said, "Do you mind if I get back to work? I have another job in an hour."

"Oh, no problem," I said. "Thanks for keeping this bed looking nice."

Aspen seemed to take that as her cue. "Yes. I'm so glad to be leaving it in good hands."

Jason gave her a slow smile. "It's a fitting memorial to my soldier relative, I feel."

Was he testing Aspen to see if she shared her brother's opposition to the memorial garden? I held my breath, unsure if she was aware of the animosity between Cody and Jason.

To my relief, Aspen said, "It's a beautiful plaque. I love that you chose such pretty plants to honor the soldier."

Duly appeased, Jason nodded and turned back to his work. Aspen, Coal, and I walked into the kitchen.

"I hadn't mentioned Jason to you yet," I said. "He and your brother were at odds over that garden, because it honored a Confederate soldier. Cody didn't want it there."

She twisted her lip, running her roller brush into the paint. "Cody never had time for history. It was his worst subject in school. I'm guessing he mentioned it to one of his Cali friends and they leaned on him to oppose it. Or maybe Tobias did. Cody wouldn't have bothered to research that soldier's story." She sighed. "I'm sure that came off as incredibly offensive to Jason, if he's a relative."

I took the painter's tape, placing a strip along a white wooden baseboard on a nearly-finished wall. "That's what I was worried about. Jason was all worked up at the garden club meeting, and his anger was definitely focused on Cody. But I can't see him doing anything rash like coming over and shooting him over a memorial plaque."

"That would be pretty extreme," she said.

Coal trotted back into the living room, settling once again by the front door. Aspen rolled the paint toward the ceiling moldings, her long arms making the job easier. She started humming, so I figured she was focused on the job at hand.

But something was bothering me. As I stroked blue paint along the tape line, I realized what it was.

There wouldn't be any dead hosta leaves this time of year.

I eased onto my feet, then stood and looked out the window. Jason was nowhere in sight.

Either that was the quickest cleanup job ever, or he'd been lying about why he was reaching into the hosta bed—the same bed where Cody had been found dead.

15

I told Aspen that Jason had a flimsy excuse for visiting the memorial bed, but she seemed unconcerned. "Maybe he wasn't talking about trimming the hostas, per se," she said. "There could've been dead leaves in another bed."

"But he was standing next to that one," I said.

She shrugged. "I figure the police will be looking into anyone who had issues with my brother. I'm sure Jason is on their list."

It felt a little like Aspen was blowing off my concern, but at the same time, I knew she was ready to leave town. "Are you flying back to Nashville after you're done here, or are you going straight to California?" I asked.

She poured more paint into the tray and coated her roller with it. "Nashville first, since I'll need to pack up my place, but then I'm heading to L.A. I've talked with Tobias' management company, and one of their other agents will be stepping into his position soon. She wants to keep me on as her client and move forward with my movie deal. I'll have to find a place to rent, which isn't cheap out there, but maybe I can stay with one of Cody's actor friends while I'm looking."

At least things were working out well for Aspen. She hadn't lost her chance at stardom. As she carefully coated the upper corner of her wall, I tried to crush the sneaking thought that maybe her brother's tragic death had smoothed her path, making it impossible for film-goers to dislike her.

AFTER SEALING paint cans and washing out our brushes and rollers, I told Aspen I was happy to order take-out from my favorite fusion restaurant.

"Thanks, but I still have some of last night's pizza in my mini-fridge." She sighed. "I just want to get back to the inn and clean up."

I grabbed the oversized *Poseidon* book. "You might find this interesting to look at tonight. Wendy Franklin was quite a big-name actress in her day."

She glanced at it. "To be honest, I only have the bandwidth for walking around the inn's gardens and watching mindless TV. You're welcome to take it back with you. I'll grab it before I leave."

Coal roused from his nap, so I snapped on his leash and muzzle. "Sure. You want me to drop by after work tomorrow to help you with the rest of the painting?"

"I'd love that. I think we can knock it out if we hit it hard. Maybe bring coffee?"

I smiled. "You got it."

As I walked home, I decided to swing by Recycled Reads, which stayed open until six. There was something distinctly comforting about the bookstore, even though I wasn't the biggest incense fan.

As we approached the door, I checked to see if pets were allowed. There were no signs forbidding it, so I led Coal inside and headed for the mystery section.

Arlo emerged from a back room and gave me a wave. "Nice to see you again, Macy." He took a step closer. "What a regal dog."

He'd chosen a good term for my Dane, who was quite sleek and self-contained. "Thank you," I said. Coal dutifully sat down and raised a paw to shake Arlo's hand.

As Arlo grasped the heavy paw, he smiled. "And he's friendly, too."

I glanced toward the side room that had once contained the book I now held. As if reading my thoughts, Arlo looked down at it.

"I saw in the news what had happened to the man who'd bought that book," he said. "I remembered his name was Tobias. Very sad. I couldn't even tell he was using drugs."

"I couldn't, either. He kept it hidden well." I held up the book. "I wondered how you came to have this particular book in your shop. Was it a big seller back in the nineties?"

He shook his head. "That's the interesting part. I

didn't realize it when I sold the book to Tobias, but Cody Franklin was the one who'd originally ordered it. He'd used the name Franklin when he called to request it, so I didn't put two and two together to know who he was. I'd sent him a text reminder to pick it up, but he never showed. I just assumed he was no longer interested. That was right before...well, it was too late."

"Did he not mention that his mother was in the book?" I asked.

Arlo shook his head. "No, he didn't. Was she an actress?"

"She was actually the star of the film," I said.

Before Arlo could respond, the door burst open. I turned to see Chancellor stalking directly toward me. The hackles went up on Coal's back.

Arlo held up a warning hand. "Hey, man, what's your hurry?" Although his voice said laid-back hippie, his eyes said "stop right there."

Chancellor seemed to pick up on the chilly vibes and slowed down. He pasted on a smile. "Macy, I was wondering if I could ask you a question?"

Since Arlo and Coal were with me, I gave a slow nod. "Okay."

"Listen, I kind of needed that job at the Franklin house. I'm not sure what Aspen told you about what happened, but I know you're close with her, so I wondered if you could put in a kind word for me."

I put my hand on my hip. "And why would I do that for you, Chancellor? I saw you two arguing. You didn't seem too keen to work for her. Plus, I heard about the truck incident this morning. Not very professional, if you ask me."

He huffed, but didn't take a step closer. I didn't have to look down to know that Coal's posture and stare were downright menacing.

"It wasn't what it looked like. When I got to the house, this guy called me over to his truck. He said he had a question, but he needed me to get in since he couldn't ask me on the street. I was about to refuse, but he offered me money."

"And marijuana?" I asked.

"No, and I swear I wasn't smoking it, either. Aspen jumped to the wrong conclusions. The guy had been smoking, sure. His truck reeked of it."

Arlo straightened some books on the shelf, presumably giving us space, although I sensed that he was ready to intervene at a moment's notice.

"You can't smooth things over with Aspen yourself?" I asked.

"She's already blocked my number."

It was strange to have Chancellor at my mercy, devoid of his usual smug behavior. He actually seemed a bit desperate. Maybe he wasn't the biggest contractor this town had ever seen.

I couldn't resist prodding a bit. "You told us you were the best contractor around. A contractor with that kind of reputation should stay booked solid."

"Times are tough, I suppose." He looked defeated. "You know, that guy didn't even give me the money he promised. He just kicked me out of the truck when Aspen walked over, then he took off."

"Do you know who he was? What did he want to know?" I asked.

"He was that same baldie with the anchor tattoo

who'd argued with Mr. Franklin. Said for me to call him 'Boss Hogg.' Kinda dumb nickname, if you ask me. He wanted to know if Aspen had the resources to pay him what her brother owed."

It just hit me that Chancellor had always referred to Cody as "Mr. Franklin," yet he called Aspen by her first name. I supposed I should expect no less from a misogynist like him. I wondered if Aspen had picked up on his lack of respect, too.

"Listen, I doubt there's any way Aspen—and 'Miss Franklin' might be a better term for you to use—would be interested in having you finish the job you so valued so little," I said. "I've already recommended someone else for the work, because I happen to know some other quality contractors in the area." As he shifted on his feet, I added, "By the way, what was your answer to Boss Hogg?"

He shrugged. "Why should I tell you? You scratch my back, then I'll scratch yours." He turned and strode out the door, letting it slam behind him.

Arlo took a deep breath. "That was unpleasant. I'm sorry I wasn't much help. I'm not great with conflict."

"You stuck around, and I appreciate that. Besides, I have my dog, so I wasn't really worried."

He looked concerned. "He mentioned a bald guy with a tattoo and a big truck. I'm pretty sure that was the man who parked in a loading zone on Saturday, just outside my store. I had to go out and ask him to move his vehicle. He was having a heated conversation with a thin little blonde woman. She gave me a death glare and said they'd get moving when they felt like it."

I was betting she was the same petite blonde I'd

seen, and now she was chatting up a drug dealer. "You didn't report them to the police?" I asked.

"I was going to, but by the time I got a chance to check out the window, they'd driven off." He looked at the clock on the wall. "I'm afraid I need to start closing up. Were you interested in buying anything?"

I shook my head. "I was just browsing. I'm sorry I attracted such bad company into your shop." It suddenly sank in that the baldie and the blondie had done their illegal parking on Saturday—the same day Cody's body was found. "What time did you see this truck?" I asked.

He glanced over from the display shelf he was tidying. "A little after noon, as I recall."

That wasn't long after we'd found Cody's body. "You might want to call the police station and ask for Detective Charlie Hatcher, then tell him what you told me about seeing those two together," I suggested.

Arlo gave a slight wince as I said "police station." Maybe he was nervous about getting involved, so I continued to press my point.

"Saturday was the day Cody Franklin was found dead. I'm guessing you saw the same blonde woman I spotted in Cody's garden, and the bald man was on the premises that day, too. Those two must be connected, and not in a good way."

He nodded. "That makes sense. I'll call and let them know right after I close up."

I led Coal toward the door and gave Arlo a parting wave. But even as he told me goodbye, the look on his face was wracked with extreme discomfort.

Did he have some kind of digestive issues? Was he coming down with something?

Or did our new bookstore owner have a problem interacting with the police?

16

The house had gotten cool, so I threw on a hoodie and made myself a mug of spice tea before settling into an castoff chair Vera had recently given me. It was an olive-colored velvet wingback that had thinned in spots, but I loved its soft texture, especially when I felt chilled. I pulled one of Auntie A's afghans over my feet and dug into my Mary Higgins Clark book again.

My phone rang, so I glanced at the screen, only to see that Vera was calling me. I picked up quickly.

"Hi, sweetie," she said apologetically. "I hate to call you this time of night, but you'd told me a guy in a truck was bothering you. Well, Waffles has been barking at some truck parked outside my house for about ten minutes now. It's been playing booming music and just sitting there with its engine running. I can't see what color it is in this dim light, but I'm hoping it's not the same one that was giving you problems."

My chill deepened. "Thank you, Vera. I'll let Bo know about it. If nothing else, it's breaking the noise ordinance."

I hung up and called Bo. By the time I'd said, "There's a loud truck outside Vera's," he was already out the door, phone in hand. I didn't have to explain that I suspected it was Boss Hogg.

I couldn't leave him out there alone, so I leashed Coal, slipped into my Crocs, and headed into my back garden. Sure enough, a truck was sitting in front of Vera's, blasting music. Its lights were out, though. The streetlight wasn't the best, but I could tell that it was a darker color.

I could see Bo's phone flashlight bobbing along toward the driver's side door. He pounded on the closed window. "Open up!"

The music grew louder as the person opened their window. I couldn't hear the conversation that took place, but a couple of moments later, Bo walked my way. The truck promptly roared off down the street.

"Who on earth was that?" I asked, walking toward my gate.

Bo stepped in, but Coal stayed next to me, like he knew there'd been shenanigans going on down the sidewalk. "It wasn't Boss Hogg," he said. "Just some guy who claimed he didn't know about the noise ordinance. Said he was from out of town. He had an Ohio plate."

"That's weird he'd choose to park where he did," I said. "But it's a free country."

"Sorry for the scare." His concerned eyes met mine. "Don't worry. Charlie hasn't stopped looking for Boss Hogg."

I pulled him closer. "I know. But I found out today that Boss Hogg and the blonde woman from Cody's garden were seen talking together in a truck just after we discovered Cody's body. That can't be a coincidence."

He agreed. "Did you let Charlie know?"

I explained that Arlo at the bookstore was the one who'd seen them. "He's likely called the station by now, although I'm not sure if the message will get through to Charlie after hours."

"I'll text him to check his messages." He placed a wide hand on my upper arm and gave it a light squeeze. "You want me to stay on the couch tonight? Or you can come over to my guest room."

"I'll be okay, but I'll probably lay off reading my suspense novel. Oh! I need to let Vera know it was a false alarm."

He opened the gate. "I hate that you're so rattled. Sleep with Coal close and that rifle I gave you closer."

"Will do." As he walked home, I took Coal inside and locked the door. After calling Vera, I decided that I really needed to hear Titan's voice. I shot him a text first, to see if he was around. The deal with dating an FBI agent was that sometimes he wasn't available to answer the phone.

There were other repercussions of dating an agent, like knowing he was doing extremely dangerous yet important work that he could never tell me about, or like understanding I had to try to hold him loosely because he was often in the line of fire. He was incredible at his job, a formidable opponent to any evildoer, but he wasn't invincible. Sometimes I wished he'd move into a desk job, but I knew he'd hate that with every fiber of his being. He was born to be a hero—even down to his magnificent first name.

Thankfully, he called me back quickly. "Hey, there," he said. "You need me?"

My heart melted. I really did, but I didn't want to admit it. I filled him in on the latest events with my truck scares, then told him how Chancellor had followed me into the bookstore. When I shared about the blonde woman hanging out with Boss Hogg, he interjected a comment.

"Hang on. You didn't tell me you saw this woman in Cody's garden. Describe her to me."

That was a weird question, but I had to assume he had some kind of inside FBI track on her, so I gave him all the details I'd noticed, right down to her sharp chin.

He let out a gust of air. "I'm going to hang up, then send you a photo. You call me back and tell me if that's the woman you saw in the garden and spa, okay?"

I agreed. A few moments later, a photo popped up. My eyes widened as I recognized the ice blonde who'd given me the pointedly cold shoulder at the spa. Her hair was in shorter bob and her cheeks were thinner, but it was definitely the same woman.

I called Titan. Without giving him time to speak, I said, "That's her."

He clicked his tongue. "Well, then, we have a problem. Because you're looking at the elusive Anne Louise Moreau."

I SLUMPED INTO MY CHAIR, wishing it would swallow me up. I'd been close enough to the ruling queen of organized crime that I could've tackled her myself, but I hadn't recognized her.

After using Bo to send her own husband to prison, Anne Louise had continued toying with my brother by making flirty calls, sending flowers, and basically letting him know she was watching his every move. She'd even wished him congratulations on becoming the town mayor, for Pete's sakes.

Fire rose inside me. "I can*not* believe it," I said to Titan, who was waiting patiently for me to process this disturbing information. "If only I would've known. She was so tiny, and completely unprotected. I could've grabbed her and called the cops. I could've busted up her whole stinking empire." An empire that encompassed plenty of drug-running and even human trafficking.

Anne Louise had started out small, fencing art and jewelry under her husband's nose. In the process, she'd developed key connections with Leo's underground network. Because she had such a knack for instilling blind loyalty in her lackeys, the FBI had gotten worried, and their worst fears were realized once Leo's empire kept running—even growing—after he was out of pocket.

And now the calculating villain was hanging out in our town—first, at a homicide scene, and then later, with a known drug dealer. I couldn't get over how small the new crime kingpin was. No wonder she hadn't spoken to me at the spa—I would've recognized her heavy Southern accent anywhere after hearing her calls to Bo.

"It's best that you don't approach her, no matter how harmless she looks," Titan warned. "It's good that you didn't catch her. She'd never go around unarmed." After a pause, he said, "I'll tell Bo about her. He needs to know she's in town."

He had anticipated my biggest concern, and I wished I could hug him. "Thank you," I said quietly. "And thanks for letting me know what we're dealing with. Will you tell Detective Tucker, too?"

"I will. Listen, I won't offer platitudes or tell you not to worry. I know you will, at least until she leaves town or gets locked up. You just keep your eyes open, like you have been. I don't have to tell you that Anne Louise has any number of minions she can call on to do her bidding."

"I feel like we're talking about Lucifer," I said grimly.

"In a way, we are. She's doing his work, that's for sure. Remember how Leo's chum was trafficking women right there in Lewisburg?"

"How could I forget? I almost joined their ranks, along with Kylie and her sister." I got chills every time I thought of the man's name, even though he was safely behind bars.

"Anna Louise has no compunctions about expanding that area of her husband's business. As you know, drugs and human trafficking play well together."

No wonder the woman's eyes looked soulless. "I hope she gets what's coming to her," I said.

"The agency is doing everything it can to rope her in. But, again, if you see her, do not approach. Don't even speak to her. Just get away and call Charlie, Bo, or me."

"I will." I shifted to a lighter topic, just to feel like Titan was close for a little longer. "What are you up to tonight?"

And with that, he was off to the races, telling me about a newfound gladiator documentary. As I listened to my boyfriend share his enthusiasm for ancient Rome, I tried not to let my thoughts wander back to Anne Louise's appearance in town, which was comparable to a lion who'd escaped the arena.

The question was, why had that *particular* lion been prowling around Cody's house?

17

That night, disjointed dreams kept me tossing, filled with spears and lions and house paint. By the time I woke, I was ready to get out of my own head and go to work. Shelter dogs would be a welcome distraction. I gave Coal a vigorous head pat, then headed through the connecting door to the cafe, since it hadn't opened yet.

Kylie had arrived early, her new sword tattoo looking foreboding under her shorter black skirt. Her eyes raked over my hair and face. I thought I'd fixed myself up enough to hide the traces of my sleepless night, but Kylie seemed to see through my façade.

"Hey, I've been worried about you." She poured beans into the grinder. "Bo told me some truck was stalking you. Why would someone do that?"

My mind flew to Boss Hogg's connection with Anne Louise. "I'm not entirely sure, but it's not something I want to happen again. I don't know if he planned to shoot me out that window, run me over on the side-walk, or what."

She turned to me, putting both hands on her hips. With her pale skin, cropped dark hair, and black cloth-ing, she looked like some alternate version of Joan of Arc. "Yeah, that better not happen again," she breathed.

Summer unlocked the door and finagled three dogs into the cafe. "We have more doggies today. And we have a frisky one, too." She pointed to a larger, light blond puppy that looked like it had more than a little husky in it. "Jake likes to run free, so you have to keep an eye on him. He also likes to nip at the big dogs."

I took his leash, and he was curious enough to trot toward the Barks section with me. I didn't want to compare the cute dog to the *other* Jake I knew, that being my dud of an ex-husband.

Summer hurried up behind me, leading the other dogs, which both looked like they had pit bull in the mix. I could feel her gaze drilling into the side of my face. "You're looking stressed," she said.

I gestured at Kylie. "Y'all are making me feel like I look like a hot dumpster fire today."

"Scorching, baby," Kylie joked.

Summer hurried to smooth things over. "You look fine. We just know you well, that's all. What's going on? Anything I can help with?"

"Not really." If I shared with Summer that Anne Louise was in town, she'd only jump on my worry train, since I was sure Bo had mentioned her.

She unleashed her dogs, and they ran into the play area. "Okay. Well, you have my number if you need it."

She gestured to Jake. "And, like I said, you have to watch that one like a hawk. One thing I've discovered is that he's very interested in treats. That might be a helpful tool."

Jake shot her a devil-may-care look, then tore around the play area in a frenzied circle. I had to laugh. "Well, he can't act any worse than the times Waffles was in here."

"It's a wonder that maniac doodle was finally able to settle down," she said. "Bless Vera's ever-loving heart for opening her home to her."

"I think it was love at first sight for both of them," I said. "And Waffles is a pretty effective guard dog. She keeps Vera posted as to any strange goings-on outside." Like the out-of-state truck blaring music last night. I winced.

Summer placed a hand on my shoulder. "Sometimes it helps to talk," she said softly.

I had to smile, since Summer was the last one to open up about her worries. She'd told me she didn't know how many of her estranged family members she'd be inviting to her wedding, but she still hadn't shared why she'd left her Mennonite background at a younger age and struck out on her own.

I gave her a quick hug. "I'm doing okay, I promise."

Her fathomless brown eyes lingered on mine for a moment. She took a deep breath and pulled herself up straighter. "All righty, then." Pointing to one of the bigger dogs, she said, "That one's called Mustard. The other one's named White. As you might have guessed, my assistants decided to use Clue board game names for this week's group of strays. Jake was a drop-off from a family that couldn't handle him on their farm. Let me know if anyone's interested and I can get them more details."

"Sounds great. I'll steer them toward the shelter."

As Summer headed out, Jake made a crazy dash for White's toy. I could tell the Barks section would keep me hopping today, which was exactly what I needed to keep my mind off the possibility of Anne Louise's continued presence in Lewisburg.

JIMMY WAS next up on dog duty, since Bristol and her mom were making a summer orientation trip to her future campus. Jake seemed calm as Jimmy approached, but the moment I opened the side door to let Mustard out, Jake bombed outside. Thank goodness the grassy plot was entirely fenced. Jimmy took the leashes and headed out after them.

I decided to grab one of Charity's new picnic-style brie and prosciutto sandwiches for my lunch, along with an iced latte. As I walked over to the cafe counter, Milo greeted me with a jaunty smile and a casual, "Hey, there." The art of respectfully greeting one's boss seemed to elude our upper-class employee, but I was willing to let it slide because I knew that underneath his cavalier exterior, he was devoted to our cafe crew. I often wondered if he didn't have a stronger bond with us than with his own driven and distant parents.

After placing my order, I moved toward the pick-up counter. The bell jingled, so I glanced over at the door. It took me a moment to realize the man in a blue

Oxford-cloth shirt and chinos was Jason Lilly, since I'd only seen him in gardening clothing.

He glanced my way, then gave me a polite nod. Instead of going to order, he strode over to my side.

"Macy. Good to see you again. I was hoping you'd be here. I wanted to talk to you about something."

I took my drink and food bag from Milo and pointed to a table. "Sure. I'll sit down and you can join me once you've ordered."

Jason nodded. As I settled in at the table, I glanced around the cafe. From the clean white bricks to the set-in fireplace to the rough wood touches, everything about the space seemed inviting. I thought again about how thrilled Auntie Athaleen would've been to see how Bo's vision had lit up our hometown.

Jason made his way back to me, steam rising from one of our cobalt blue Fiestaware mugs. Bo and I had scoured online sites to stock up on vintage mugs in the welcoming blue shade, and it felt good to highlight a West Virginia-based business with our own.

As Jason sat, he blew at the foam on top of his drink. I took a couple of sips of my vanilla latte, waiting for him to speak.

Finally, after taking a hesitant drink, he met my gaze. "That's a great macchiato," he said, his tone approving. "Listen, I was thinking about something, and I wondered if I needed to tell the police about it. Since you seemed to be friends with Aspen, I thought I'd ask you first."

Aspen? What could she have to do with anything? I leaned against the chair back, trying to brace myself for anything. "Sure. Fill me in."

"It's just that I saw her at her brother's house that morning—the morning that he died. I wouldn't have thought anything of it, but I just read in the online news piece that she claimed to be at the Greenbrier spa all morning."

My mind whirred as I tried to lock the shifting pieces into place. "Wait...*you* were at the house that morning, too? I wasn't aware of that."

"I already told Detective Hatcher about it. I had to drop by early to top off the mulch in the memorial bed. It was a quick job, so I was in and out. But as I headed back to my truck, I saw Aspen standing on Cody's porch. This was when she was supposedly at the spa."

Surely Charlie had checked into Aspen's alibi, hadn't he? "It sounds like something you should tell the detective," I admitted. I didn't want to throw Aspen under the bus, but why had she clung to her story that she'd been at the spa all morning?

Jason nodded and took another sip. "That's what I was thinking. Like I said, I just now realized that's what she was saying."

Feeling more comfortable with the landscaper now that he'd opened up to me, I decided to be candid with him. "I have a question for you. What were you really doing in that hosta bed yesterday?"

His eyes widened. "You noticed that." Setting his mug down, he leaned in closer. "I was trying to rectify a little mistake. See, Abigail's eyesight isn't what it used to be. When I was mulching the morning of the tour, I realized she'd planted a baby hosta where a dinnerplate needed to be. I came back yesterday to replace it with a bigger one that wouldn't stand out like a sore thumb."

I doubted that anyone would've noticed the discrepancy in size, but I respected the fact that Jason had been sneaking around to protect Abigail's feelings.

He glanced at his phone. "I'd better get going—I have a landscaping consult with a new hotel over in Fayetteville. But I'm glad I caught you. I'll call Detective Hatcher after my meeting." He set his empty mug on the table and stood.

"Thanks." I started gathering my things as he walked away. I wished he hadn't told me about Aspen's lie, because that meant Bo had been right to caution me about her. I didn't want to entertain the possibility that a sister could shoot her own brother, yet she'd been at Cody's house the morning he died, contrary to what she'd said.

18

I was sure the detective would soon get the entire scoop from Jason, but in the meantime, it wouldn't hurt if I checked in with Aspen and touched on the topic of her Greenbrier spa trip. I texted to see if she was painting at Cody's house, and she responded with a brief "yes," probably because she was messy from painting.

After telling Milo goodbye, I headed up the sidewalk to the Franklin house. There was something forlorn about the unfinished place. Recalling Chancellor's desperate plea to put in a good word for him, I felt an unexpected twinge of compassion. Maybe he'd been telling me the truth and he actually needed the work. Maybe he hadn't been smoking weed in Boss Hogg's truck. But how could I possibly recommend him in good faith? The bottom line was that I didn't know him well enough to determine what kind of person he was, outside of an in-your-face flirt.

When I knocked on the door, Aspen called out from the kitchen. "Come on in. It's unlocked."

Trying to mentally gear up for the conversation I needed to have with her, I slowly stepped inside. Once I reached the nearly-finished kitchen, I took a moment to admire the smooth look of the walls.

I crouched down beside Aspen, who was painting above a floorboard. "You've done great work. Look at those clean corners."

She turned my way and grinned. She was wearing the same paint-covered shirt she'd worn yesterday, but she'd managed to keep her face relatively paint-free. "It was largely thanks to you. What's up?"

I wasn't quite ready to jump into things yet. "Have you heard anything from Detective Hatcher?" I asked.

She balanced her brush on the paint tray. "Nothing. But I plan to call him later and ask if I can't go ahead and book a flight. My new manager is telling me I need to get out to California as soon as I can, and I want to do the memorial for Cody."

"I'm sorry the autopsy is taking so long. It has to be frustrating." I stood and leaned against a counter. "I was wondering—what treatments did you get at The Greenbrier? I've thought about going there sometime. Were they as good as the salt spa?"

"I just did a detox body wrap, so I can't compare apples to apples, but it was fun. First they do a dry body brush, then they use some kind of warm algae to pull out toxins. I got a scalp massage at the end, too." She sighed. "I'd love to book one now to relax after all this painting, but I need to be saving up for my move. Cody paid for the detox wrap."

"That sounds like a long process."

"It was just fifty minutes," she said.

The home and garden tour had started at ten in the morning, so presumably the club ladies had showed up by nine thirty or so to set up. They'd seen Tobias around that time, but no one after that. I should've thought to ask Jason how early he'd dropped by.

"What time do they open over there?" I asked in my most innocent tone.

"Oh, you have to book it ahead of time," she said. "Their hours vary. My appointment started at nine."

It only took about fifteen minutes to get from town to The Greenbrier. So Aspen could very well have paid an early-morning visit to her brother before the garden club showed up.

There was nothing for it but to ask her for an explanation.

A little voice inside my head told me it might be risky to question a possible murderer's alibi, but I shoved it down. I was standing some distance from Aspen, and if she tried anything, I could be out the back door before she got to her feet.

Plunging right in, I said, "Listen, I need to ask you something. Jason stopped in at the cafe this morning, and he said he saw you talking with Cody early on Saturday. I figured he was mistaken, but it sounds like you actually had time to drop by here before your detox wrap."

Her eyes hardened, and she pursed her full lips. "Surely you're not suggesting that I killed Cody, are you?"

I met her gaze. "I can't really believe that of you, no.

But I can't understand why you'd fail to tell Detective Hatcher you were here."

She stood, and I sized her up. While she definitely had extra height on me, I more than made up for that advantage with my weight. Given just the smallest start, I knew I could crash into her middle and tackle her to the ground. I'd played enough football with my brother to make an educated guess about whether or not I could successfully body-slam someone.

"No. I didn't kill Cody." Her every word sounded weighted. "But you're right—I didn't tell the detective I'd stopped by that morning, either." She reached for the counter, so I stiffened, but she was simply retrieving her phone. She opened it and scrolled down, then turned the screen so I could see it. "This was Cody's last text to me."

I hesitantly took the phone and read over the brief text. "Come over this morning before spa," he'd said. "I found some of my mom's letters in a wooden box that I want to show you. Important."

She shook her head. "I couldn't understand what on earth he was talking about. What could his mom's letters possibly have to do with me? But he sounded pretty worked up, so I dropped by around a quarter to eight." Her eyes didn't swerve from mine. "I promise you, he never answered the door, even though I kept knocking and ringing the bell. Jason must've noticed me while I was waiting on the porch. I swear to you, *I never went in the house*. That's why I didn't mention it to the police. I knew it would look incriminating, but I never even saw Cody that morning. If I told the detective I dropped by, it would only confuse things and point him away from my brother's real killer."

"You don't get to pick and choose what you tell the police," I scolded. "You know Jason has to tell Detective Hatcher what he saw, now that he knows you lied about your whereabouts."

She set her phone down, then held up her hands. "Look, I understand. I'll tell the detective the same thing I told you." She took a step closer, waving a finger toward the living room. "But here's what I want to know —what happened to those letters? The minute the police let me into the house, I looked all over for them. But I couldn't find a wooden box or letters of any kind. That tells me someone probably took them. Now I'll never know why Cody insisted I come over."

She made a good point. Cody had urged Aspen to come over right away and look at the letters, so they might hold a link to his murder. "Do you think Cody might've found some unique hiding place for it? Sometimes these older houses have secret nooks," I suggested.

"I've searched the attic, the basement, and in all the closets. While it's possible there's some hiding place I've missed, I have no idea where it could be."

I had an idea. "I know this sounds lame, but maybe Chancellor found some hideaway areas when he was renovating. You could give him a call."

Her lips flattened. "Ugh. Over my dead body."

Regardless of how we felt about the contractor, we needed to be certain the letter box wasn't still in the house before Aspen put the place up for sale. I reluctantly said, "I could call Chancellor, if you want."

She shrugged. "Go ahead. But I've already been in touch with the contractor you recommended, and he's coming over tomorrow. I hope to give him Cody's house plans, then start packing up." She dusted her palms together. "I'm washing my hands of this place. I don't need constant reminders of my brother's murder."

I could understand her sentiment. "I get it," I said. "But don't you need closure as to why he died?"

"The autopsy—whenever it gets done—will probably tell us a lot," she said. "I hate to say it, but it was probably drug-related, just like Tobias' death."

"I guess that is what it looks like." After all, we knew that drug lord Anne Louise Moreau had been in town, hanging out with Boss Hogg, who was doubtless one of her underlings. And Boss Hogg had been asking if Aspen could pay off her brother's debts. What else could he have been talking about? The sooner Aspen moved out of Boss Hogg's territory, the better.

"I'll call Chancellor," I said. "And you need to get in touch with Detective Hatcher."

Her look softened. "I'm sorry I wasn't completely up-front with everyone. I just didn't want to bog down the investigation. I'm grateful for all your help."

I gave a brisk nod and headed for the door. I could easily put myself in Aspen's shoes. If I'd been in the same position, I might've withheld information so police would go after the real killer instead of focusing on me.

But the harsh reality was that Aspen hadn't told *me* the whole truth, and I had a problem with that. I'd thought of her as a friend; someone who needed my help. But I'd been betrayed before, and I'd determined not to trust the wrong people again.

I'd try to locate the letter box, but that would be the extent of my efforts. It was time for me to step aside and stop trying to comfort a sister who had already written her brother off, anyway.

19

B ack home, I curled up in my velvet chair, took a deep breath, and called Chancellor. He picked up on the first ring. "I've been waiting to hear from you," he said.

Whether he was referring to his proposed date with me or to Aspen's response to his desperate work pleas, I wasn't sure. In either case, I had to disappoint him.

"Aspen will be going with someone else for the renovations, like I told you at the bookstore," I said firmly. "But she has a final question for you."

He started to protest, but I rolled right along, determined to get what I wanted. I was now operating in my "stubborn mode," which had been known to thwart even my relentlessly driven brother. My unwillingness to bend supplied me with limitless creative reserves to accomplish the task at hand.

"Now, I know you're the type of stand-up guy who wants to keep his reputation clear in this town. You can either answer one simple question, or I'll make sure your name is mud for the way you acted toward Aspen, and I'll throw all my references toward Ash Hyatt. Don't underestimate me, Chancellor."

He huffed around a little, then finally said, "Okay, okay. What's your big question?"

"Did you find any nooks or crannies in Cody's house where something could be hidden? Loose floor-boards, moving wall panels—that kind of thing?" Coal walked toward the back door, so I stood to let him out.

"What? This isn't the Hardy Boys."

"Just answer the question, please."

He grunted. "Nothing like that. The only loose floorboards were the rotten ones we had to pull up. I hope Ash can handle all Aspen's repairs. That house is the gift that keeps on giving."

He'd effectively put the kibosh on my theory of a hiding place. Maybe I *had* been reading too many mystery books. "Thanks, Chancellor. I won't blacklist you when people ask about contractors, but I do recommend you work on your interpersonal skills with your clients. That's the way to get repeat customers and build your business."

"Well, la-di-da, aren't you just the cat's pajamas?" His voice was dripping with sarcasm. "Thanks so much for your expert tips, Macy. All the best with your stupid dog cafe." He hung up on me.

Maybe I'd overstepped with Chancellor, but if he actually listened to my advice, he might be able to succeed as a contractor.

After letting Coal back inside, I texted Aspen that Chancellor hadn't run into any hiding places. She responded that she'd already gone back to the inn, anyway. She thanked me for my efforts, but her message seemed more clipped than usual.

So that was that. I wanted to clear my head, so I decided to walk over to Summer's apartment and pick up some lime green hostas she'd separated for me. Coal was eager to come along, so I leashed and muzzled him and we headed out. Summer always knew how to put my mind at ease, and I could use a little real friendship right now.

SUMMER WAS STANDING by a sprawling garden bed, holding a white cat. She maintained her landlords' beds in return for a discount on her garage apartment.

The moment the cat noticed Coal, it turned into a blur, tearing over Summer's shoulder and making a manic dash toward the side of the garage.

Rubbing at a spot where the cat must've clawed her, Summer said, "That's Casper. He loves being out in the sun, but he's scared of his own shadow. He's my current foster kitty."

She knelt by the flowerbed, pulling out a cardboard box laden with baby hostas. "They're spreading so fast, I wound up digging all of them up except for one. I wanted to make room for that purple beebalm you gave me."

I hated to point out the obvious. "You know that spreads like crazy, too."

She nodded. "I know, but the butterflies love it so much. I'll keep an eye on it and pull up the shoots." She stepped over to pet Coal. "Good to see you, boy. You keeping your girlie out of trouble?"

As Coal leaned in for a scratch, Casper inched his way back to the flowerbed, creeping around the remaining hosta.

"I've been good, I promise," I said. "But I got into it with someone today."

Summer's eyes widened and she grabbed the hosta box. "It's getting hot out here—let's go over to the back porch and sit in the shade."

With Coal in tow, we headed for the back of the garage, where Summer's landlord had built her a small porch with a swing. Mr. Maynard doted on Summer as if she were his own child, and so did his wife. I knew the older couple had harbored the hope that Summer might marry their bachelor son Rex, but they'd continued to shower her with kindness even after she'd gotten engaged to Bo this past Christmas.

I caught Summer up on my adventures of late, and, as I'd expected, she said all the right things.

"I know I'm a transplant to Lewisburg, but from what I've heard, Chancellor is burning bridges left and right." She kicked off, pushing our swing into motion. "He took over that business from his dad, but he's running it into the ground. He cussed Mr. Maynard out for asking him to pick up bricks for the porch *he* was building, if that tells you anything about his character. You were doing him a kindness to warn him to shape up."

"I can't imagine anyone having a decent reason to cuss Mr. Maynard out. And yeah, thanks. I hope my advice gets through to him." Coal yawned and pressed against my leg as Casper crept along the edge of the back flowerbed.

"And Aspen," Summer continued. "Who does she think she is? Miss Hot Shot Movie Star? You've given her more than enough of your time and effort. I say good riddance, and have fun in L.A."

It cracked me up how Summer already acted like a watchful big sister, even though she was only a year older than I was.

"It's okay. I don't feel like we're ending on bad terms," I said. Smacking a hand to my thigh, I said, "Oh, shoot. I need to get that book back to her before she leaves."

"What book?" Summer asked.

I told her about the coffee table book that Tobias had bought. "You need to come over and watch that *Wife of Poseidon* movie with me sometime," I said. "You'll see where Cody got his acting chops. His mom was really talented."

"I'll bet." She stopped the swing. "How about I run inside and make us some lemonade?"

"You're sweet, but I'd better get back. Coal will need his water bowl soon."

Hearing his name, my Dane rose to his feet. Casper, who'd been blissfully rolling in a sunny spot on the grass, tore into the flowerbed and hid under a leafy bleeding heart plant.

Summer placed a hand on my arm. "Oh, I forgot to tell you. Jimmy called and said that a sweet lady came in and connected with Jake. She's bringing her husband to the shelter tomorrow, so they can decide if they're ready to adopt him."

"That sounds promising," I said.

She nodded and led me to the front yard. Passing the box to me, she said, "Enjoy the hostas. And don't stress about Aspen. You've done all you can for her."

I supposed I had. But as I walked Coal up the driveway, I couldn't shake the feeling that I'd missed something. I could only hope I'd think of it before I returned Aspen's book, because I doubted I'd see her after that.

20

My Friday night was low-key, which was nothing new—I tended to be a homebody, unless my friends had things planned for me. Bo stopped by after work to drop off some taco meat, and I could tell by the crease in his freckled forehead that he'd heard about Anne Louise.

"Titan told you," I observed.

"I wish I'd known that was the blonde you saw in Cody's garden," he said. "I didn't get a good look at her, since I was focused on the body."

"Understandably so." I opened the taco container and inhaled. "Smells wonderful. Thank you, bro."

"I made my own seasoning, since there's less salt that way. Doc Stokes said my blood pressure was inching up into an unhealthy zone."

I scrunched up my nose. "I don't know how that's possible, since you go running practically every day."

He shrugged. "He said it's genetic, so that means

you might need to check yours periodically. I didn't realize Dad had high blood pressure, too."

We both fell silent, trying not to get swallowed up in the gaping hole left by our parents' premature deaths. I busied myself by turning on the oven and cutting open a package of hard taco shells.

"It doesn't help to know that Anne Louise might be on the loose in town—or should I say in *your* town, Mr. Mayor." I glanced back at him. "You want some?"

He shook his head. "No, thanks. Summer's coming over to watch a movie, so we'll be eating at my place."

"Sounds fun. I love you, bro. Try to relax tonight, and thanks for the tacos."

He gave Coal a final pat and headed out. I sat down in my green chair, waiting for the oven to heat. To kill time, I grabbed the coffee table book and started glancing through the photos. Most of them were in color, although several black and white scenery shots had been scattered throughout.

I stared at the portrait-style photo of Wendy Franklin. Her intense, long-lashed eyes pulled you in, and she wore her Greek garb like royalty, making her the perfect choice for a sea goddess.

When the oven beeped, I dashed over and put my taco shells in. After setting out some shredded cheddar, sour cream, and salsa, I headed back to my chair. Coal was already curled on his pillow, but he watched my every move, as if wondering if he might have a nibble of the beef Bo had dropped off.

"It would be too spicy for you, boy," I said. "Remember that time I gave you buffalo chicken dip? You couldn't get enough water to wash out the taste. We don't need a repeat of that." I jumped up and grabbed a dog treat, then tossed that to him instead.

Digging back into the book, I read up on some of the other actors. Most had been relative rookies to the industry—except for the leading man, George Stanuk. He'd been a supporting actor in several 90s films, but *Wife of Poseidon* had been his big break.

I personally thought he'd botched the job. Although he was tall, dark, and handsome, he'd delivered most of his lines without feeling. The only thing that had seemed to wake him up was kissing Wendy. I could think of several 90s actors who could've pulled off the role of Poseidon better.

It was surprising to find that several pages had been dedicated to the lead actors' body doubles, but it made sense, given some of the dangerous stunts they'd filmed. Wendy's double was shown on the side of a boat, preparing to dive in with the sharks. "Opal was known on the set for her fearlessness," the caption read.

Opal was such a pretty name—I'd thought the same when I'd met Opal from the garden club. Auntie A's birthstone was an opal.

I flipped the page to find a photo of Wendy's double, pointing her raised toe toward the edge of a rocky cliff. Her tan skin glistened beneath a flimsy Greek tunic, and she was laughing toward the photographer. She looked ready to take on the world.

But the moment my eyes fell to the caption beneath, I gasped.

"Tragedy struck with Opal's high dive into the waters of the Aegean. The scouting crew had failed to identify several hazardous rocks near the shoreline."

I held my breath, turning to the next page, which showed Opal being shifted onto a stretcher. The horrified faces of the actors surrounding her said it all.

"Opal was rushed to the hospital, but her injuries were irreversible," the caption read. "Her spinal cord was damaged, forcing her to be confined to a wheelchair. To honor her fearlessness, her cliff scene was retained in the movie, but her entry into the water was spliced in from an earlier dive."

This was getting a little eerie. Opal Tustin was also in a wheelchair, although I didn't know why.

My oven beeped again, so I ran over and loaded my tacos. Grabbing my plate, I rushed it over and set it on the table next to me. I took up the book again, frantically scanning for a last name, even though Opal's surname likely would've changed by now.

But there it was, under a beautiful portrait of her on the very last page. "We dedicate this book to Opal Tustin. May she forever be remembered for her courage and contagious happiness."

If it *was* the same Opal Tustin, she'd apparently never married. And she'd settled in Lewisburg, West Virginia.

Why hadn't Opal mentioned her connection with Wendy Franklin to the police? Had it been too traumatic to bring up?

There was only one way to find out. I called Vera, asking if she had a list of garden club members' phone numbers. She said she did, and when I asked for Opal's number, she readily gave it to me. I noticed a lilt in her voice.

"Are you doing something special tonight?" I asked.

"Randall's over," she said. "We're playing Trivial Pursuit, and he's trouncing me." She lowered her voice. "I don't mind, though."

I smiled. Vera's romance with the retired railroad worker wasn't exactly hot and heavy, but it was encouraging to see how they genuinely loved spending time together. I felt a unexpected stab of loneliness. Both my brother and my neighbor were with their significant others this Friday night, and here I was, calling up a garden club lady to ask about her past.

Once I'd wished Vera a good night, I considered whether I should hold off until tomorrow to call Opal. It was seven fifteen and, although it was still bright out, maybe she went to bed early, like Matilda. I recalled that once Auntie A had hit her late sixties, she'd sworn by going to bed at eight.

I examined the photo of stunt double Opal Tustin. Her eyes danced and she had a warm smile, as if she were living life to the fullest. I couldn't tell if her features matched up to those of garden club lady Opal Tustin.

It probably wouldn't hurt to call her, mention the book, and ask if, by any remote chance, she'd ever been a body double. It would only take a *yes* or *no* answer, and we could go from there.

After several rings, Opal picked up, her voice filled with uncertainty. "Yes?"

"Hi, Ms. Tustin. This is Macy Hatfield, from the cafe. I came to your garden club meeting."

"Oh, yes, it's lovely to hear from you. I get so many calls from telemarketers, and I wasn't sure who would be calling me from South Carolina."

I'd kept my old cell number when I moved back to West Virginia, but it tended to confuse people. "I'm sorry. I just kept my old number when I moved back."

"Of course you did," she said, as if that were the most logical decision in the world. "It was lovely to have you visit our club the other day. I do hope you'll consider becoming a member. We need younger blood." She chuckled. "I wasn't sure if I could man the garden table this year, but Abigail looked after me."

She'd given me an easy opening into my motive for calling. "Ms. Tustin—"

She interrupted me. "Please, call me Opal, dear."

"Will do. I'm sorry to bother you about this, but I've come across a book that has a lady with your name in it. I was wondering if that might be you. She was a body double in Hollywood."

"Isn't that fascinating? I'd love to see it. Would you want to bring it over now? I'm sitting out on my front porch."

"Oh, sure." I hadn't really planned on dropping by, but she seemed so eager. "Where do you live?"

"I'm right over by Matilda—just three houses down from her, on the left. It's a gray two-story with a light wood door. There's a row of red peonies lining the edge of the yard."

I realized she must own the house that backed up to the wooded area behind me. "That's not far from me. I'll walk over in a few minutes," I said.

It was only after I'd hung up that I realized she'd never given me that simple *yes* or *no* answer. Had she been Wendy Franklin's stunt double, or was I barking up the wrong tree?

21

After scarfing down one of my tacos, I placed the remainder of my meal in the microwave until I could get back and polish it off. I considered bringing Coal along on my short walk, but he would probably intimidate the wheelchair-bound lady.

I wondered if I'd jumped the gun—after all, if Opal had been Wendy's double, showing her the book would only bring up traumatic memories. Although she'd likely have her own copy of the book, since it was dedicated to her.

But if that were the case, why would she ask me to bring it over? She would already have one.

By the time I walked past the lush peonies up to Opal's porch, I'd convinced myself she couldn't be the same woman. She was curious as to how someone with her name had been in Hollywood, that's all. The fact that she was in a wheelchair didn't mean she'd suffered a spinal cord injury. She probably had trouble getting around for some other reason.

Opal's white curls bobbed as she greeted me. She sat in a cushioned chair with her wheelchair close by. "Macy, how wonderful you could come." She gestured to an old-fashioned metal chair. "Please, have a seat. I'm so curious about this book. Would you like a glass of mint iced tea?"

It would probably be a hassle for Opal to make her way into the kitchen, so I shook my head. "I just ate, but thanks." After setting my phone on a nearby table, I extended the Poseidon book toward her. "This is the coffee table book I'd mentioned. I'm sure it's a coincidence that this woman has your name."

She took the book with trembling hands and placed it in her lap. After staring at the cover for a long minute, she said, "I've been looking for a copy of this for years, ever since I lost mine." When she looked up, tears had welled in her eyes.

I took a deep breath. "You mean...you're *that* Opal Tustin?"

She nodded, carefully turning the pages until she reached the photo of her fateful cliff dive. She tapped a wrinkled finger to the page and whispered, "The day time stood still." Glancing up again, she asked, "Where on earth did you find this?"

"You won't believe it, but it was in the new bookstore in town—Recycled Reads. Strangely enough, Cody Franklin ordered it not long before he died. His manager found it and bought it for Cody's memorial service."

She blinked back tears. "Poor Cody. He passed too young, just like his mother."

"You must've known his mother quite well, to fill in for her as a double. Did you look exactly alike?"

Shaking her head, she said, "Goodness, no. Just our hair color and build. The cameras don't zoom in on the doubles, which is for the best. My features weren't like hers. She had a small pout; I had a wide smile. She had a short nose, and mine was longer. You can see her eyes were dark as cocoa, but mine were hazel."

I could tell that Opal had spent quite a bit of time measuring herself against Wendy Franklin.

"But you were so adventurous," I said. "Were you close to Wendy? What was she like?"

She flipped to the page with Wendy's glamorous portrait and stared at it. "She was practically other-worldly. Kind of like Elizabeth Taylor, with men falling all over her. Even George..." Her voice trailed off, and she seemed lost in the past.

"You think something was going on with her co-star?" I asked.

Opal seemed to come back to herself. "I don't like to spread rumors. There's plenty of that in Hollywood." Her eyes searched mine. "But you don't seem the sort to gossip. Yes, I felt certain that George and Wendy were carrying on together. Why her husband didn't guess it, I don't know, but then again, he hardly visited the set. When he remarried so soon after Wendy died...I confess, I had my own suspicions." Her lips flattened. "They *said* it was a heart attack—that she had a preexisting heart condition. But I always wondered if her husband hadn't gotten sick of her flings and decided to get rid of her."

"You think he killed her?" I asked. "Did you tell the police, or did they even consider that angle?"

She shook her head. "They never looked into it, probably because our studio executive didn't want any negative press, and he was well-connected. I was just starting therapy when Wendy passed, which was soon after the movie released. I had no desire to stay involved in that world."

I hated to ask for details on her dive, but she seemed ready enough to talk about it. "You hit a rock below?"

She gave a slow nod. "A bank of rocks, actually. The impact caused a lumbar spine injury, which affected my hips and legs. If it would've been any higher, I might've been completely paralyzed, like Christopher Reeve. I suppose I should be grateful."

I wasn't sure how to respond, so I just nodded, waiting for her to speak again.

"They used some experimental therapies to restore my mobility." She gave a forced smile. "As a stunt double, at least I had top-tier insurance."

"Did they work well for you?" I asked.

She grimaced. "They did initially, so I can't complain. I was able to walk for many years. But as I grew older, arthritis complicated everything. Although I can stand and sit on my own, I can't walk more than a few steps at a time." She gave a defeated sigh. "I'm actually considering hiring someone to help me out during the days."

"I'm so sorry." My thoughts flew to Della, who sat with invalids all the time. "I have someone I can recommend, if you're interested."

She fell silent, clinging to the large book as if it were a lifeline. Her gaze wandered to the distant mountains, which the sun had draped with bright ribbons of pink and orange.

I considered how difficult Opal's life must have been. After chasing her Hollywood dreams, she'd suffered unspeakable personal loss, the kind that had dogged her throughout her life. Had she ever married? She hadn't mentioned a husband, and she'd retained her last name from her body double days.

I admired her for staying active in the home and garden club. At least she hadn't let her injury steal all her joy. I would make a point of dropping by her place regularly; maybe bring her treats from the cafe on my lunch breaks.

Shadows started to blanket the street. I glanced at her short sleeves and said, "It's getting chilly fast. Do you want me to wheel you inside?"

She seemed to startle back to the moment, rubbing at her bare arms. "Why, yes, now that you've offered. I'd appreciate that. I might need a bit of help."

She set the book down on the table and I moved her wheelchair over. She showed me where to park it, and then, using her arm strength, she transferred herself into the seat. Once she'd repositioned herself, I handed her the book and rolled her chair toward the door, where I gently worked it over the metal threshold.

I flipped on the light in her darkened hallway, and she pointed to the right. "My reclining chair is right there in the living room, if you wouldn't mind taking me that way."

I wheeled her in and helped her settle into her chair. "Would you mind if I kept this book?" she asked.

"Oh, I'm sorry, but I told Aspen she could have it for Cody's memorial service," I said. "I'd planned to drop it off tomorrow, since she's heading out of town soon. But feel free to look at it until tomorrow morning—I can pick it up then."

She fumbled with the drawer on an antique side table. "I don't want to inconvenience you. Let me just get my reading glasses and look at it a few more minutes."

Hoping to offer her a bit more privacy, I began to look around. Unlike Matilda, Opal had chosen tasteful furniture for her living room. She had several antiques, including a marble-topped dresser and a roll-top desk.

Her bookshelves were stuffed with hardcover editions, and I was guessing that reading was her favorite pastime. But I didn't see a framed photo or family album anywhere.

Spotting a leather-bound copy of *The Great Gatsby*, I stepped closer to examine the gold-leaf stenciling along the spine. As I turned to ask if I could pick it up, I froze in place.

Opal hadn't budged from her chair, but she was holding a small revolver in her hand and pointing it at me. If I had to guess, I'd say it was a .22 caliber.

Exactly like the one that had sent a bullet through Cody's chest.

"I truly hate that it's come to this," she said. "You really are such a nice girl."

22

The ridiculous scenario seemed like something out of one of those daytime dramas Auntie A used to watch. I couldn't believe it was real, but I raised my palms anyway, since that seemed the only option.

"I don't understand," I said.

She blinked. "You don't? I figured you had talked with Tobias."

"Tobias? No, I barely spoke to him at all." What did Tobias have to do with anything?

She tapped on the book. "This book was one of the last things linking me with George. I've spent years hunting down each copy and destroying it. But somehow Tobias got his grubby hands on this one. He planned to use it against me as blackmail."

I looked like a big target standing in front of the bookshelves, but I was afraid to move. "You're saying this book can be used as blackmail?"

She gave a brief nod. "It had that photo—the one of George and me. He was kissing me, you see. We were in the background, behind the dazzling Wendy, so most people wouldn't have noticed."

I didn't understand what was so scandalous about George kissing Opal. "So you liked each other?" I asked.

"Liked?" she croaked. "No, George *loved* me. We had plans. We were going to travel the world together. But then I had my accident. While I was recovering, Wendy swooped in and stole him from me."

I'd noticed that George and Wendy definitely had sparks in *Wife of Poseidon*. But had that been before or after Opal's devastating dive? Had he been carrying on with both women at once? I wouldn't put it past a Hollywood star. But Opal sounded convinced he'd only had eyes for her.

She seemed to be losing her grip on the gun, and it dipped toward the floor. But even at a crooked angle, there was no way I could dodge a bullet if she pulled the trigger, since I was standing directly in front of her. I should probably ease onto the couch and make myself a smaller target, but any movement might set her off. And I'd left my phone on the porch.

Trying to keep her talking, I said, "I'm sure no one would know about you and George, especially since there aren't many books left." I couldn't understand why their romance was even an issue.

"There were letters, too." She rested the gun in her lap. "Somehow, Wendy got hold of the ones I'd sent George." She twisted her lips, and hatred filled her eyes. "I heard her mocking my devotion, saying I was nothing but an ugly West Virginia hillbilly, and that George could do so much better."

I cringed at the words. Wendy had been cruel, then. And willing to have an affair. "I'm sorry," I said.

"It wasn't enough for her to steal him. She had to twist the knife when I got wheeled into the advance screening of the movie. She whispered that he had never loved me; that I was delusional. She said she'd report me to the police if I kept bothering him." She absently patted the gun, and my body tensed. "But I was presented with an opportunity later that night. A glass of champagne...I knew George would come running back to me, once she was out of the way."

Was she confessing to murdering Cody's mother? I couldn't even process this information, so I turned back to the most recent deaths.

"What does any of this have to do with Tobias, or even Cody? He was just a child when his mother died," I said.

She angled her head, like an actress preparing for a close-up. Everything about this encounter was surreal. Here I was, standing in a garden club lady's tastefully decorated living room, listening to her casually tell me about murdering someone.

"Don't you see?" she asked. "Cody bought that house so he could snoop on me. I even saw him walking past my place a few times. I got the feeling he suspected I had something to do with his mother's death, even though she had a heart problem, which is why she took the nitroglycerin." She grinned. "I guess she shouldn't have left her tablets in her purse that night."

So now I knew how Wendy Franklin had died. I wished Opal would take her eyes off me, even for a moment. It might give me the chance to run into the hallway.

She sighed. "I knew I needed to talk to Cody, so I made sure to sign up to greet the tour guests at his house. I wanted to show him I wasn't scared of him. I headed over there early that morning—I had one of those Uber cars drop me off." She looked downright proud of her resourcefulness.

I shifted just a bit, and she tightened her grip on the gun.

"Cody was surprised to see me there so early, of course," she continued. "But he asked if he could roll me into the house because he wanted to show me something. I recognized his mother's wooden box sitting in his living room, and he started pulling letters out of it, telling me he'd figured things out. He said he knew I'd been obsessed with George, and that I'd killed his mother for her affair with him." She gave a bitter laugh. "I told him he'd gotten the wrong impression. I wasn't the one obsessed. George loved me just as I loved him. It was Wendy who was obsessed. She just wouldn't let him go."

My heart sank. "You shot Cody, then?"

She shrugged. "A wheelchair-bound older lady like me has to carry some kind of protection, in case some jackwagon tries to take advantage of me. I always keep my revolver tucked into my chair bag. I grabbed the gun and fired it at him, but it didn't knock him to the ground. He staggered around, shouting at me that I wasn't going to get away with it." She seemed devoid of emotion over killing such a young man. "Luckily for me, he said he was going to get help, and he stumbled out the back door into the garden. He fell down on the grass."

"But how did he wind up in the hosta bed?" I asked.

Her eyes flashed. "Like everyone else, you believe what you see." With the gun in one hand, she began to push up from her chair. It didn't take long for her to draw herself into a standing position. She looked a bit wobbly, but she aimed the gun at me again and continued talking. "I can still walk a little. And I have a good upper arm strength—always did. It's what made me such a great stunt actress. Still, it took plenty of effort to wheel across the lawn, then maneuver Cody's body into the hostas. I had to roll my sleeves over my hands so I wouldn't leave prints. Afterward, I tucked my gun into the chair bag, rolled myself over to the visitor's center, and waited for Abigail to pick me up, just like we'd planned." She rubbed her arms. "I didn't have much strength by the time she wheeled me to the tour table."

"What did you do with the letter box?" I asked.

"I took care of that later. See, garden club members had access to Cody's house bathroom." She sank back into her chair, keeping her revolver at the ready. "It was easy enough to go in and get rid of them."

Opal's heartless, calculating actions were so at odds with her benign looks, I was having a hard time convincing myself this wasn't some elaborate act. But she was giving me all kinds of details that fit with Cody's murder.

She didn't seem in any hurry to shoot me, but, barring some kind of outside interruption, I couldn't see how I could make it out of her living room alive. In desperation, I asked, "Do you know anything about Tobias' overdose?"

"Overdose," she scoffed. "Nothing of the sort. I did that myself."

I blinked. "But—"

"You're wondering how an old crip like me could get rid of that scum. Well, let me tell you, it can be done. Several days after Cody's death, Tobias asked me to the inn for lunch. He said he had something to discuss. It turned out that Cody had told him about the letter box and the book he'd ordered. He said he was gathering proof that I'd killed his mother. Tobias was a drughead, but he was sharp enough to suspect me of Cody's murder and think that he could blackmail me for it. I told him I wouldn't discuss it in the inn's dining area, so he wheeled me back to his room." She chuckled. "Can you imagine, the prey escorting the predator to its room? He had *no idea* what I could do."

Keeping one eye on the gun, which was once again resting in her lap, I tried to distract her further. "You threatened him with your gun and had him overdose?" I guessed.

She gave me a devious look, as if we were playing a fun game. "No. I noticed his drug paraphernalia when he wheeled me past the bathroom. When he walked over to open the blinds, I said I had to use the toilet and headed into the bathroom before he could intervene. He rushed in after me, trying to pick up his stash. In the meantime, I grabbed a couple of needles, shoved them in his arm and depressed the syringes, and waited for him to drop. I didn't expect him to *die*, of course. I just wanted to retrieve the book, since he told me he'd picked it up from the bookstore. When he woke up, what could he possibly do about it? Tell the police I'd used his own drugs on him?"

She heaved another sigh and picked up the revolver. "You know, Macy, I really hate to do this. But I can't go to prison at my age and in my condition. All those deaths are water under the bridge—retribution, if you will. Wouldn't you agree that I've been punished enough?" She wheedled as badly as my great-uncle Hubert when he tried to justify another late night at the bar to my aunt.

Once again, I raised my hands. "Listen, Opal—"

Clomping footsteps sounded on the porch steps. There was a heavy rap on the door, then the doorbell started ringing as if someone were holding it down.

This was my one chance. I made a wild dive over the couch and fell to the floor, out of Opal's sight.

23

A muffled, British-accented voice sounded from outside. "You all right, Opal? I noticed you had your porch light off, and you always keep it on. I wanted to make sure it hadn't gone all dodgy on you." The doorbell buzzed again. "Maybe you're just knackered, but if you don't open up, I'll feel obliged to call for help. I don't like you living all alone over here," she scolded, as if she, too, didn't live by herself.

I heard Opal move, and I hoped and prayed she didn't open fire on the couch. "I'm fine, Matilda," she called out hoarsely.

"You don't sound it." Matilda tried the doorknob and it gave. She stepped into my range of view, wearing her heavy, rubber-soled boots and a trench coat. "I told Abigail I'd check in on you, since you didn't call her tonight." She walked into the living room and drew a deep breath. "Oh, no," she breathed.

Had Opal turned the gun on Matilda? Irritating as the woman was, I couldn't stand by and let her get shot.

I jumped to my feet. "Stop it!" I shouted.

Matilda screeched like a banshee and flung her hands in the air. Opal, who was pointing the revolver to her own temple, began shaking. "I can't go to prison," she moaned. "You have to understand."

I shot Matilda a desperate look, which somehow seemed to galvanize her into action. "Now, now, Opal. No matter what you've done, you can always find forgiveness, isn't that what you told me once?" She took a couple of steps toward Opal, making her hand tremble even more. I was afraid she'd drop the gun and it would go off.

Even if I made a mad dash for the revolver, there was no way I could reach it in time. Once again, I felt like I was stuck in some kind of far-fetched TV drama —the kind of show where Matilda Crump was determined to be the hero.

She clomped another step forward, still trying to coerce her friend into putting her weapon down. "You think this is the answer, but really, it isn't," she said. "I don't know what you've done, or why this youngster is here"—she made a wild gesture toward me—"but shooting yourself isn't the solution. And it's in very bad taste, Opal, I must say. You ought to know better, having grown up Presbyterian."

With a slow movement, Opal brought her other hand to the gun. I held my breath, but instead of pulling the trigger, she lowered it to the table beside her. "I'm sorry, Matilda," she said. "You're right. I can't go out this way. It's not who I am."

Matilda plodded the rest of the way over and gave

Opal a hug. Holding her arms around Opal's torso, she turned back to me. "Call the police," she hissed.

I rushed outside and grabbed my phone. After what felt like minutes of fumbling, I managed to pull up Charlie's direct number and call him. Once he'd promised to come over, I called Bo, telling him where I was. I had a feeling he'd blaze a shortcut between his back yard and Opal's house.

Although I wanted nothing more than to run for the hills, I couldn't leave the surprisingly valiant Matilda alone. With my phone in hand, I walked back into the living room.

Matilda jerked her head toward the side table. "Grab the gun," she ordered.

It was only after I had the revolver in hand that I realized Matilda's British accent had faded into a West Virginian one. In any other circumstance, I would've found this lapse hilarious.

Footsteps sounded on the porch and Bo shouted, "Macy!"

"In here. Everything's okay," I assured him.

He charged through the open door, walking strangely. I glanced down to see that he was wearing only one flip-flop, and his other foot was bare. "Lost one on the way," he said briefly. He looked at the revolver in my hand, then turned to Matilda and Opal. "Now, somebody had better tell me what's going on."

It didn't take long to get Bo up to speed, and by that time, Detective Hatcher and a couple of officers had arrived on the scene. As they wheeled Opal toward the front door, she reached for me. For some reason, I extended my hand, allowing her to squeeze it with her cold, strong fingers. "It wasn't about you, dear. You're a good girl." She gave me a sad smile. "Love is a hard taskmaster, that's all."

Matilda had taken a seat on the couch. As she spoke to an officer, I realized she wore a long nightgown under her trench coat. She must have noticed Opal's light was out on her way to bed, then come scurrying over. I wouldn't be surprised if she didn't make a nightly visual sweep of the neighborhood to verify nothing was amiss. But her busybody ways had basically saved my life. I shot a smile at her, and she responded with a disapproving frown. I supposed we'd gotten back to our normal uneasy terms with one another.

My phone rang, and it was Aspen. "Detective Hatcher told me someone confessed to my brother's murder," she said. "He wants me to come to the station. I knew you'd want to know."

"Thank you. I was actually here when she confessed," I said. "I've given my statement to the detective, so he'll fill you in. Just let me know when you're flying out—I want to get Cody's book to you before you go."

I said goodbye and nodded to Bo, who'd stuck around while I was giving my witness statement.

"You ready to head home?" he asked.

"Just a sec." I headed over to Matilda. "Thank you for what you did. I'll never forget it. You'll have free coffee at Barks and Beans for life."

She adjusted her thick glasses. "I don't drink that sludge, pet. Only tea for me." Her British accent had reappeared. If anything, it was even stronger than before.

"Free tea, then." I forced a smile.

She sniffed. "Indeed." Turning back to the officer, she said, "Now, where was I?"

On Saturday morning, Aspen asked if we could meet at Cody's house, so I grabbed the Poseidon book and headed over. It was a relief to see that Ash was already busy on the renovations.

When Aspen opened the front door, I said, "It looks like the place is in good hands."

She motioned me inside. "Ash has been so helpful —even suggesting things I hadn't thought of, like listing this place with a rental agency. It would be nice to make some income on it before I try to sell it."

I handed the hard-won coffee table book over. "I found the photo of George kissing Opal," I said, turning to the page. In the picture, Wendy was the central figure, but far behind her in the crowd, you could make out George leaning forward, giving Opal what looked like a peck on the cheek.

"She was worried about *this* incriminating her?" Aspen asked. "That doesn't make sense."

"None of it does. Why would she kill a young mother in the first place?" I sighed. "I didn't realize until they hauled her away that she never said what she did with your brother's wooden box of letters."

"She found it in this house?" she asked.

"Yes, but I don't know what happened to it. She said she dodged into the bathroom during the home and garden tour, then got rid of them, whatever that means."

Aspen looked thoughtful. "I guess she could've flushed the letters down the toilet. But then where did she hide the box? We looked everywhere."

I considered for a moment. Opal had managed to tote a revolver around in her wheelchair bag. What if she'd shoved the box in it, too? After all, we didn't really know how big the box was. She could've slid it into her bag, then headed out to work the garden tour table. But someone might have noticed a bigger bump in the bag, and she wouldn't have wanted to draw attention to it.

I considered Opal's talent for thinking on the fly. "Hang on," I said suddenly. "We've looked everywhere *inside*. But we didn't check the flowerbeds."

She looked doubtful. "I'm sure the police did."

"They would've checked near Cody's body, sure. But what about the front beds—the ones closest to the garden table?" Recalling the rainbow array of phlox, I headed out the back door. Next to the thick patch of flowers, I got onto my knees, feeling around under their leafy stalks. Aspen joined me, plunging her hands into a patch of daylily leaves.

My fingers brushed something blocky, so I slowly wrapped my hand around it and pulled it out. It was a medium sized, carved box with a small lock on it.

Aspen's eyes widened. "Maybe she *didn't* get rid of the letters. I'll bet she couldn't get into it." She got to her feet. "I'll get a knife so I can try to pop the lock."

After working the knife around in the flimsy lock, Aspen was able to pry it open. A small stack of letters sat inside, so she pulled them out to examine them. Each one was addressed to George Stanuk at a California address.

She picked up the top letter and read it aloud. "My dearest, I think of you every night and day. Every time our eyes meet on set, I know you want to be with me. You might deny it, but I know the truth. We will travel the world together, seeing the sights and making unforgettable memories. I know you've said you loved Wendy, but you aren't seeing things clearly. All you have to do is ask me to come over, and I'll explain all my feelings to you. I know you will be mine forever. All my love, Opal."

I read a couple more, and each one was similar to the first. "I think she was a stalker," I said finally. "She was upset when Cody called her 'obsessed.'"

"He would know what a crazed fan looks like," Aspen said. "He had one woman who threw a chair through his window to get to him. She claimed to be the mother of his child, which of course, she wasn't."

"Cody realized how dangerous someone like that could be, so he put two and two together." I folded the letters back into the envelopes. "He was aware that his mother had been involved with George; I'm sure Hollywood gossip told him as much. I'm guessing that when he came across Opal's letters, he recognized the desperation—even madness—in her words. By the time Opal showed up at his house, he'd ordered the photo book to check for more proof." I shook my head. "Even if he'd lived to pick the book up, he probably would've missed the photo with George giving Opal a peck. Yet it's that very picture that proves that George *wasn't* in love with her."

"It's so twisted," Aspen said. "She seemed like such a sweet lady."

"I know. It was terrible that she had that diving accident, especially since it could've been avoided if the site had been scouted properly. But after that, she doubled down in her delusions, and her jealousy drove her to kill Wendy. Then she proceeded to kill anyone who might point a finger at her for it." I shivered. "She was ready to kill *me*, even though she claimed she didn't really want to."

Aspen nodded. "I'll give this box to the detective. My flight is booked for tomorrow, but you know what? I'm going to miss being here—and mostly because of you, Macy. I feel like you've been a true friend to me." She glanced up at the house. "Who knows. Maybe I'll rent this place out so I can come back and visit—once I become a rich and famous star, of course." She laughed.

I smiled. "Feel free to come back and spend your big bucks at the cafe."

Aspen's phone buzzed, and she glanced down at it. "Hang on. I got a text from Detective Hatcher." She scrolled down, then she looked up at me, her face crumpling.

"What is it?" I demanded, grabbing her arm. "Are you okay?"

"My brother didn't have drugs in his system," she said. "He wasn't using—he'd told me the truth."

I pulled her into a hug as she cried tears of joy. "I

should've believed that he wanted to change. I shouldn't have doubted," she sobbed.

"It's okay," I said, patting her back. "You knew his history, and that made it really hard to believe him."

She pulled away, sniffling. "Thank you. For everything."

I gave her a parting hug and she squeezed me tight. The contentment on her face showed she finally had closure in her brother's death.

But something bothered me as I walked away. Why had Boss Hogg showed up at Cody's house that day, and why had he been asking for payment, if Cody hadn't bought drugs from him?

I guess we'd never have answers, if the police couldn't locate the dealer...or his boss, who was doubt-less Anne Louise.

As I rounded the corner of the cafe, I stopped short to see a black truck parked on the curb by my house. I could hear Coal barking from inside. I quickly typed in the license number on my phone, then called Detective Hatcher. While I was on the phone with him, I walked into the cafe and grabbed Bo.

My brother ran out just as a bulky bald man stepped out of my garden gate. It had to be Boss Hogg.

Bo ran straight for him, tackling the man to the ground before he could register his approach. As the Boss tried to grab for something in his pocket, Bo rammed an elbow into his forearm. "Stay still or I'll break your arm," he breathed.

I leaned in toward the front window of the cafe. Jimmy caught sight of me, and I motioned him outside to help Bo. He walked out quietly, so the customers weren't alerted to the fact that something was going on outside.

Together, Jimmy and Bo kept the bulky man pinned to the ground until Charlie and an officer arrived. When I told them I'd seen the drug dealer exiting my gate, the officer stepped into my back garden to look around. A few moments later, he came out carrying something in a gloved palm.

"This was in front of your door." He walked over and opened his hand. "Any idea why he'd leave that for you?"

I stared. It was a small pink salt rock. In black permanent marker, someone had written, "Until next time."

"It has to be Anne Louise," I said.

Bo raised his eyebrows. With steel in his voice, he told Charlie, "You can lock this joker up. He's a little fish swimming with a big shark." He met Boss Hogg's hostile gaze. "And it's time to reel her in."

I COULDN'T RELAX the rest of the afternoon, even though Coal stayed close. While I knew it was a positive thing that Boss Hogg had been caught in the act of delivering Anne Louise's twisted little message, she was still out there.

Titan called around eight. "Sorry I couldn't get in touch sooner," he said. "Bo told me what's been going on. I know it's a small consolation, but getting Boss Hogg off the streets is a big deal, especially for your part of the state."

I thought of Charity's story of her run-in with the drug dealer. "I know. He's ruined plenty of lives." Coal gave me a needy look, and when I nodded, he climbed up onto the couch next to me. Although he took up two of the three cushions, I welcomed his comforting presence.

"There's something I still don't understand," I said. "Why was Boss Hogg asking Cody Franklin for money when he wasn't buying drugs?"

Titan said, "That much, I can help with. Boss Hogg said he'd been sent to collect money from Cody, even though he'd never personally dealt to the guy before. The unpaid tab was for drugs Cody had gotten years before, in California. When word got out Cody had moved here, the Boss was sent to collect on the outstanding debt."

"That's why he showed up on the garden tour, too?" I asked. "He wanted to get payment?"

"He hasn't answered that question yet, but we think he might have been dropping something off—possibly the heroin for Tobias."

I patted Coal's soft back. "But once they'd found Cody's body, how could Tobias pick it up?"

Titan sighed. "That's where we have to fall back on guesswork. We know that Tobias somehow wound up with heroin that he couldn't have transported on his flights. We know that Anne Louise was also in Cody's garden that day, long after Boss Hogg was there. We're wondering if Anne Louise took the tour to scout things out, then noticed Cody's body before you did. She'd know that police would sweep the area, so she probably retrieved the heroin stash and escaped through the fence. She could've delivered it later to Tobias."

Leave it to a criminal like her to be the first one to sniff out a murder. "But why was she in Lewisburg in the first place? Was she so invested in Tobias?"

"He'd be a valuable client, especially if he was distributing her product to the rich and famous. So yes, she might've wanted to meet with him herself."

How Anne Louise managed to run a nationwide crime network boggled the mind. Her husband's drug empire had stretched all the way to California, which is where Cody had stumbled into it. Now that Anne Louise had taken over, she seemed to know more about the criminals in our small town than the police did.

"One more thing," he said. "Charlie ran those prints from your bookstore owner, Arlo Edwards. Since they weren't in the system, he asked me to dig around a little. We were surprised to find that someone with his exact name and social security number died of childhood cancer at age five."

"What are you saying? Is Arlo crooked?" I couldn't mesh that with the friendly hippie who'd called Tobias out on his rude comment.

"We don't know, but we're looking into things. Just be careful around him, that's all."

Yet another person I needed to be wary of. I heaved a sigh.

Titan jumped in. "I want to lighten your load somehow. You've had so much going on—it must've been terrifying to be alone with that unhinged woman while she was pointing a gun at you. I know there's not much I can do from here—"

"Then come visit me," I said impulsively.

He didn't even hesitate. "Sure. Just tell me when."

I thought a moment. "Next weekend, we'll be setting up our coffee booth at the Renaissance Faire just outside town. I'd love it if you could visit and hang out with us. Maybe you could stay with Bo, or stay in that cabin you've rented; do some fishing if you like."

I could hear the delight in his voice. "I love Ren faires! My mom used to make us costumes and give us a day off homeschool to go to Medieval World every fall. I'll ask for the time off."

"Medieval World?" I smiled. "And what did you dress up as?"

"I think it's properly known as 'cosplaying' these days." He chuckled. "But I'm not telling. Who knows— maybe I'll reuse one of my costumes for this illustrious event."

When we said goodbye, I leaned back on the couch. Despite the insanity of last night, I felt very loved.

Coal gave a happy whine, and I said, "Yes, boy, you'll get to see your friend Titan soon. And, thank goodness, so will I."

You can now preorder Heather Day Gilbert's
next Barks & Beans Cafe cozy mystery,

KNIGHT BREW

**Welcome to the Barks & Beans Cafe, a quaint place
where folks pet shelter dogs while enjoying a cup of
java...and where murder sometimes pays a visit.**

The Barks & Beans booth at the Renaissance Faire is
hopping, since Macy managed to talk her muscled
redhead brother into donning a kilt for the occasion.
Even better, Macy's boyfriend Titan has come for a
visit, so she can't wait to peruse the shops and watch
the shows with him.

But when a well-rehearsed joust takes a fatal turn, Macy becomes a key witness. Can she believe her eyes, or did someone cloak their ruthless intent with smoke and mirrors? A late night stakeout seems the only way to determine what really happened...but someone scarier than the plague doctor is lying in wait for Macy, and this time, the damsel might not find a way out of her distress.

Join siblings Macy and Bo Hatfield as they sniff out crimes in their hometown...with plenty of dogs along for the ride! The Barks & Beans Cafe cozy mystery series features a small town, an amateur sleuth, and no swearing or graphic scenes. Find all the books at heatherdaygilbert.com!

The Barks & Beans Cafe series in order:
    Book 1: No Filter
    Book 2: Iced Over
    Book 3: Fair Trade
    Book 4: Spilled Milk
    Book 5: Trouble Brewing
    Book 6: Cold Drip
    Book 7: Roast Date
    Book 8: Shade Grown
    Book 9: Knight Brew
    Standalone Mystery: House Blend

Be sure to sign up now for Heather's newsletter at **heatherdaygilbert.com** for updates, special deals, & giveaways!

And if you enjoyed this book, please be sure to review online and share with your friends about this series!

Thank you!

ABOUT THE AUTHOR

Heather Day Gilbert has been a "dog person" ever since she was nine years old, when a stray dog named Brownie showed up at her family's doorstep. Growing up, Heather considered Brownie one of her best friends, and, like Macy, she's had a dog in her life ever since. Many of the dog and cat antics in the *Barks & Beans Cafe* series are drawn from real-life experiences (unfortunately, the washing machine flooding incident with Stormy in Book 4 was all-too-real).

This series is based in the real town of **Lewisburg, West Virginia**, which has been voted "Coolest Small Town in America" by Budget Travel. Heather and her husband regularly visit the quaint town to do on-the-spot research for the *Barks & Beans Cafe* series.

Heather's also an avid Agatha Christie fan, and would love to someday own all her books. Her favorite Agatha mystery is *Ordeal by Innocence*.

Heather enjoys conversing with her readers via her email newsletter, and she occasionally weaves her readers' dogs into this series as shelter dogs.

Sign up for more dog and book discussions, West Virginia photos, and all the latest on the *Barks & Beans Cafe* series at heatherdaygilbert.com!

Printed in Great Britain
by Amazon

33800369R00108